Memoirs of Hizaion
Volume 1: Sentinels of The Invisible

D.McNeele

2015

www.facebook.com/Hizaion

First printing: August 2015
ISBN 978-2-9552200-2-3
© Cover Aline Mieze

Chapter 1

The child, barely twelve-years old, nodded, her senses numbed by the smoke around her.

"So?"

The priests hung on her every word. Her eyes rolled back, as a hoarse rattle emerged from her throat. She opened her mouth, and a voice spoke as if from beyond the grave:

" Born will be a child who shall seal the Iron Age

Temple destroyed, magic returned

While man hesitates to conquer the dawn

The Destructor will rise

All the stars will fight amongst themselves

The comet

Sign of the storm, it will announce the light of Ashera."

The priests looked at each other. This prophecy had already been pronounced 50 years ago under the reign of King Hizaion.

"Oracle, tell us now. This prophecy is already taking place. But what about after ? What happens to the Caste of Priests, your protected ones? Oracle, I order you to speak to us !"

The little girl began to sniff, and her head contorted to an odd angle. Her wet hair stuck to her eyes.

"I see nothing; from the blackness of the earth ravaged by dark light, will spring forth the lost flower of Sabians."

The little girl sat on a stool, breathing vapors that rose from a slot in the ground. She let out a throaty growl and fell forward with a thud. No one made a move to touch her, except for a priest who approached and asked anxiously:

"Will we survive, Oh gods?"

At that moment, Wyre entered the room: the girl froze.

"Aman ordered everyone to gather and prepare to leave the city. What are you still doing here?

The oracle is about to complete another prophecy.

- We don't have time! Where did you find this child?

- She's a novice. She has a gift for the oracle. She delivered the prophecy of the Destroyer... from the Sabians.

- She's too young to be submitted to the oracle."

Wyre walked over to the young girl's body. She searched for her pulse, but dropped her arm as a trickle of blood appeared and rolled down her parted lips towards the ground.

"Oh gods, forgive us ..." murmured Wyre, closing her eyes.

Never had a human being died in the service of the oracle, and now had to be tonight ... The priests looked at her body, frightened, reluctant to leave.

"Take care of the body.

2

- Should we bury it in the mound under the tree with the rest of the Caste?

- I don't know..."

Wyre was suddenly very tired. She had no idea how they would get away. All their efforts at reconciliation with the population now seemed futile. Faraoh was a much better strategist than

them in the public arena.

"It's just that... the troops gather there.

- Then find another place in Samatya that can accommodate the body of a novice and go. We have to evacuate the city and join the City of Rosendal."

She got up, wiping her forehead, beaded with sweat from the bonfires, and quickly left. She would have to tell Aman about the incident. Even a novice beneath their ranks counted in these troubled times. They had lost so much during the persecutions by the populace.

The men held hands and began to pray for the soul of the deceased. One turned red with confusion and embarrassment fidgeted, wringing his hands. When Wyre was far in the corridors of the temple, he cried out:

"Nobody can see this body. Quickly, I know where to hide it!"

Don't make a sound. Hold your breath. Morràn progressed in the tunnel. She stopped halfway. The guard passed before the entry into the warhead that stood out in the dark night, just as she had calculated. She had exactly four minutes to mount her horse and disappear behind the alley. There, invisible to the guard of the walkway, she would follow the line of closed shops and move towards the east gate. When the tip of his spear disappeared from the crack in the door, Morran leapt toward the stables. She had to leave town quickly.

The hooded figure came in from the east gate of the city. Morràn's plan proceeded as she had hoped. She waited to cross the bridge, then launched her horse into a gallop. She knew she could slow down as soon as she passed the plain and reached the river. She would have to go easy on her horse in order to reach the south of Hizaion safe and sound. She clutched her bag of meager provisions against her chest. She could recognize edible berries from those that were poisonous. She knew the way through the chaos of Oltahisar. She knew how to avoid the mountain of the Sokars, the
reptilian warriors of the night with stone eyes. Yes, she would survive. She had survived the interrogations of the City over the past few months, as the feeling of an ever-tightening noose had

4

become unbearable. So unbearable, that she had risked tonight. Despite her young age, she did not believe in the luck of the elven armed

forces. She had seen the true nature of Faraoh, and the weapons he was preparing. They weren't up for the challenge. Nobody was, except perhaps with the help of very ancient magic. And this magic survived far from Samatya. He could not control everything. It would take years to control all the lands of Hizaion.

She clasped the medallion between her hands. She would guard this precious gift and pass it on. She chose a long gray coat that covered nearly the entirety of her mount. She was hoping to blend into the gray night and its shadows which ran towards the plain, flattened by the wind. It would have taken the keen eye of an elf to distinguish the frame walking in the heart of the dark night.

Suddenly, on her right, the horse sensed movement.

He flattened his ears, lowering his head to slow down. Morràn felt her heart racing, and dug her heels into him. What could be out here? She'd taken a small dagger, but she didn't even know how to use it... When she heard a whistle, Morràn dove towards the ground, crying out in fear. The horse lurched forward. Shaken by the frantic gallop Morràn thought, "This is impossible, I'll never make it."

She was suddenly struck by an idea. She veered her horse to the left. There, the Etheldrede forest! The horse resumed its blazing speed. She risked a look over her shoulder, and was met with the sight of two shadows that moved with the speed of eels. They could only be Sokar warriors. Morràn screamed—they were only a few feet away. The horse reared towards the branches, throwing her to the ground. Rising painfully, she threw a stone at the horse as it trailed off, followed by the two bloodthirsty creatures. Morràn threw herself among the branches, determined to reach the heart of the forest. If she could not reach the south immediately, she could at least find shelter for a few months within Etheldrede. She felt blood running between her legs: she fell on her back. The impact seemed to have been enough to trigger childbirth.

Aman, alone in the upper room of the temple Samatya, was on an out-of-body journey. Only Sabians and their army could save them. They had left the land of Hizaion months ago to reach their sacred island to the east. Would princess Vindhara hear his call?

When his spirit reached his limbs, she came towards him, haloed by light in the night. Aman knelt down in front of her as she stared.

"Princess, thank you for having me. This is serious. The Caste of Priests is asking you to intervene. Your army can change the course of the battle that will soon be raging.

- The humans have chosen their destiny. It is not for us to impose our power.

- But so many lives will be sacrificed, so many innocent people!

- The people elected Faraoh. They must assume responsibility for their choices and pay the price of what they call freedom.

- But the Elves, the royal family, they'll surely be exterminated ! The power of Faraoh is not of this world and our magic is limited against it.

- Have faith Aman."

She offered him her hands, which he pressed against his heart and kissed. She disappeared taking the darkness with her, as the Sage entered. Wyre looked at him in silence, waiting for his orders. Aman sighed:

"They aren't coming. We must leave."

- Aman... Something happened. The priests spoke to the oracle through a novice," she said in one breath.

Frowning, the Sage leaned forward and stretched the skin of his forehead with his fingers. These cursed prophecies were just the powder keg. Everything that was happening was perhaps the fault of the Sabians.

"And?"

The question shocked Wyre. Did he know the response of the novice and her sad fate?

"She's dead."

- Damn... Where are the priests now?"

The oldest stood guard at the corner of the street. If anyone came, they were done for. Crossing the forum and reaching the canal had been easy under the cover of darkness. But the sun was about to rise. Streaks of dawn were creeping into the sky. The body solemnly wrapped in a dirty cloth made a terrible noise as it plunged into the water.

"The current will carry the body out of the city. This episode will soon just be a bad memory," said the priest with the poorly-trimmed beard.

The one who stood guard replied, approaching:

"May the gods protect us."

With horror, the three individuals, shoulders drooping with anxiety, watched the body bob up to the stagnate surface. The current wasn't strong enough!

"Who goes there?"

They turned franticly, seeing three shaggy and quite rowdy onlookers heading towards them.

"Well, well... the rag-tag priests..."

One of them was a type of giant with a pointed beard, eyes sunken back in their sockets, and armed with a club that dragged along the ground.

"Come on, break one of their skulls, we need a good laugh this morning."

One of the shaggy priests waved and tried to attack the giant with a spell but he crashed his club on the priest's face. The latter collapsed in a shower of blood and a gurgling sound. In a split second, the giant grabbed the other two, and the blood-thirsty drunkards sneered. Suddenly, the first widened his eyes at the canal.

"What the..."

They rushed to capture the floating package, caught in the channel between two pieces of wood.

"Fucking rag-tags... You can't help yourselves, can you, eh! Take the kids from their families, rape them, use them for your fucking sect, and just leave them like that.

- It's not what you think! Squeaked the oldest.

- What we *think* is that we're going to destroy you and your friend."

He gestured to the giant to seize them by the feet. The two priests clawed the ground in a desperate effort to escape their future torturers, groaning when they saw the shaved-head individual pick up the giant's club.

"But first we're going to make sure you never again have the urge to cast any spells with those scabby hands of yours."

The alley of Samatya channel echoed with the sounds of cries and broken bones.

How long had she been walking ? It felt like hours had passed, as she felt herself faltering. The sweet and beneficent Magic Forest of Etheldrede had protected her by diverting the Sokars warriors. She believed in that.

"By Dana, I must find shelter."

When thunder growled, Morràn accelerated, moaning, clinging to the branches that tore at her belly. Perhaps she would find a cave, or the home of the Caste. Prayer snippets escaped her lips at full speed, while sweat beaded on her forehead. There. On the left, an easier path, brighter. How times had changed: once she could go through these woods without being worried about a thing. And now she was crawling in the dark, red eyes and muddy dress torn, desperately racing through the forest. The storm was raging, and lightning bit the sky with sudden cries. Morràn arrived at the edge of a clearing. Stones littered the floor. There before her, a pyramid was cut under the crack of lightning: the tomb of Hizaion! Tomb of the first human king, the first temple, where all royal dynasties were buried, elves and human. The door, wet from the pouring rain, was ajar and a gleam shone inside. The Sabian people were supposed to have left the temple they occupied in part. Maybe someone was still there? She rushed to enter. When Morràn was inside, the door closed behind her, as if to bury her, and the child she was carrying.

Chapter 2

Aman understood that the worst was yet to come, when, attracted by the clamor of the crowd he glimpsed through the forum window. It was then he saw the two priests hanging by their feet in the public square, their faces bloodied.

Aman held Wyre back from going out on the balcony, grasping her arm.

"It is too late for them.

- So our magic is worthless?

- Not to fight the population. And besides, they're too many of them. I'll negotiate with Faraoh to preserve the rest of the Caste and hopefully we can leave peacefully today."

Agaric stopped him. He would negotiate, and he would demand a hearing in front of the Queen.

Faraoh hated dawn. He preferred the night, when he could lock himself in his laboratory at leisure, finally free of the paperwork and vicious circle of bureaucracy and official documents. He hummed a victorious tune. The crowd pressed towards the gallows, where the two poor idiots were hanging.

"Quarter them! Quarter them!" Chanted the crowd, drunk with rage.

12

He went out on the gray-streaked marble balcony. He savored this moment, the palpable electricity in the air. He raised both hands in a gesture of appeasement:

"My brothers, my sisters, we cannot succumb to hatred. An honorable girl died because of them! They will be punished. But not barbarically. We are done with these manners of another age. You are better than that."

Passion animated his face and body. He had never needed to recite this speech because he believed. His faith was stronger than that of the priests. It was his faith in a new world that allowed him to get to where he was standing today. He gestured, and in the guard tower, which had been partially destroyed, the large piece of cloth that covered the weapon was removed. Murmurs of admiration ran through the assembly.

"Today, we are entering a new era! An era of renovation, where we rid ourselves of the past!"

The people began to clap while the gigantic parabola and its barrel pivoted toward the center of the forum. The militia onlookers parted from the platform. Half unconscious, the lipids beneath their skin began to heat up, as a result of the wave-inducing weapon. After a few screams lost in the clamor of the crowd, the two priests were only two halves of charred flesh.

"People of Samatya, do you trust me?"

The crowd roared in appreciation.

"Listen to me! Outside an army of bloodthirsty creatures is ready to invade the city and make it rain fire and blood! These foul creatures do not want humans in this world, because for them, we are monsters. They want to eradicate us!"

Faraoh let his words resonate in the anxious silence. Thanks to him, they were hanging on his every word.

"I Faraoh, I am committed to the Queen, and to protect this kingdom. Today I pledge to protect you from this army and the man in black who has sown terror for too long! Their abuses and terror expire today! Rape, murder, looting—enough! The alliance with the magical creatures is no longer enough for them! I offer this invicible arm to you, Oh people!"

The congregation clapped her hands with joy.

"Stay in the walls of the city and go home, you will be safe. With my great knowledge, our victory is assured!"

This time, it was jubilation. Faraoh inhaled this wonderful energy that always galvanized him.

"A new era opens before us!"

He disappeared from the balcony. Each piece was in place. Soon would come the delightful denouement in this delicious piece of theater, in which he played God, resolving this atrocious, but

14

necessary situation.

The young woman clung painfully to the rough edges of the rocks. She could make out narrowed eyes, a room, a floor covered with tiles and surrounded by ancient statues of kings. At their feet, withered roses that would soon crumble to dust.

"I don't understand….light…there was someone ... I'm sure." The wind howled now and released an ice storm that rushed through the cracks of the door. Morràn leaned against a wall with a shudder: the birth was imminent. Would it be a boy or a girl? She gasped, panicked and worried.

"I'm too young, I don't even know how ... How did I get here?"

She stifled a sob, "If only Mother was here, she'd know what to do."

Everything in her fought to block out the pain. She calmed herself and tried to listen to her body, now dripping with sweat. It'd be the one in charge now. She closed her eyes. This forest was holy. Etheldrede was the heart of the world, it was what they recunted to the children at night before they slept. She felt the cool stones still

wet the previous day. She was beginning to understand her body now, and listened to every spasm of her tortured belly. A shudder shook her. She sat up, her teeth chattering: there had to be another room, more sheltered. A snarling pain slashed her stomach as she threw herself forward to reach the innermost part of the room. This time, she could not suppress a cry in the darkness. The forest rustled in fear, lurking around every living being, sensing what was taking place within it. Morràn exhaled, groping in the dark, her tight clothes clinging to her icy skin.

There: the steps under her hesitant feet. The blood pounding in her temples. She had to try. She climbed the three steps, slowly, saving her strength. Another contraction gripped her belly. She lost her balance, but caught the wall with her hands. She tightened her lips, fumbling for the wall to find the door. Closing her eyes and leaning her forehead, she ran her fingers along the wall. She felt rows of sinewy lines engraved, carved into the rock, probably inscriptions. Quickly, she began to make some of them out.

"Mirror ... souls ... myrth ..." she whispered.

Then she pressed her lips together, focusing on the exhaled breath of her nostrils, leaning all her weight and her meager force on what she hoped was a door. Suddenly, a flood escaped from between her thighs. Her water broke. The stone door swung gently. A few steps ... She and her child would be better there. The pressure of the coming baby became more urgent. It was nearly crowning. She climbed the few steps that separated the room as the door closed behind her, and walked painfully to the center of the room. She crouched awkwardly, as gently as she could, her heart pounding.

She looked around her: a mirror stood before her, half silver, half tree, bathing the room in a soft blue heat. Morràn, tired, watched herself for a few seconds as she was pale, dirty, her face drawn. But the child would wait no longer. She unhooked her coat and spread it on the floor between her thighs, preparing to welcome her child. She lifted her skirts, squatting, waiting to catch her breath. If she lied down, she wouldn't have the strength to rise.

"Everything will be fine ..." she said aloud, hoping to reassure herself.

And suddenly she contracted all her muscles, and pushed with all her might, while thousands of invisible blades grated lower abdomen. She felt as if her whole belly was being torn. She gasped, leaning on her hands, her back arched. It wasn't the right position, but it was too late. She took a breath, looked up to heaven in silent prayer, and in a last effort and in a stream of blood, the child was born. Morràn, exhausted, trembling, sweating, took the baby in her arms, weeping with joy, and fell on the floor.

"Just a moment to rest…"

It was a girl, and she was already screaming. Morràn laughed ...
She held her in her arms, this little being that had stirred so much in her. She took her time to contemplate; perhaps it was her maternal instinct that kicked in. After months of misunderstanding, doubtingabout her condition. Two arms, two legs, two eyes ...

Everything was fine. She lay on the floor and hugged the little girl against her

heart. This part of her. Did she look like him? She was already restless ... Maybe she would inherit my character ... Or maybe his own ... She drove away this thought and looked at the ceiling. It was dark and too high to perceive the details, but strangely, it sparkled. Morràn indulged in the silence: the room was so quiet as if out of time. She closed her eyes and began to hum an old song from her childhood.

"The Daikini placed a crown,

On the young girl in flowers,

And its wings were open,

But were they those of Daikini?"

It was a little cold, but she could do little more than shake her daughter against her. What name could she give her? A name came forth in her mind ... But perhaps it would offend the goddess? ... No. It was a name that would protect her. She murmured:
"Andraste, Andraste ... as my daughter shall be thy name ..."
She wanted her daughter to hear ... At that moment, she called the goddess:

"O goddess, the protector

Fortify her with courage in combat,

Place on her head a crown of Faith,

Let your Virtue guide her way,

Right to her fate.

Welcome her to your bosom, warrior goddess

I put her back in your hands."

The child nestled in her mother's arms turning on her back and gazing at the twinkling stars lighting up the walls of the room. Her eyes wide open, she saw majestic arabesque contours and colors appear. It was as if they shimmered and sparkled, revealing secrets in the setting of the night. The walls and their inscriptions came to life. Carvings left there by the Sabians. Was it their prophecies that she had heard so much about? Morràn listened to the rustle of ancient words in her head, carved in the stone for eternity, resonating and calling her soul. She knew now she would not live. She had lost too much blood.

"Why?" She wept.

The baby snuggled against her breast, looking for a little of the heat that was beginning to leave the body of the young woman.

"Thus I will not see you grow up ..." she whispered, kissing her, her face bathed in tears.

"Someone will come and find you. If not a priest then a Daikini or Sabian. Someone will come. The goddess will protect you. You will have a lot to learn without me. I know you won't fail the task ahead of you."

Her voice faded to a whisper: She unfastened her medallion and placed it around her neck. She was leaving, caught by the other world and murmured:

"You have to fight to live, Andraste. But you are protected and loved, do not forget. Do not forget me."

And in a last whisper she caressed words of love, she threw her head back, no longer seeking to hold on to that little exciting life that moved gently against her breast. Morràn passed away inciting the gods and goddess of war in particular, this last plea:

"Oh protect her and let her destiny fall under your mercy. I beg you ... "

Her voice was lost like a breeze through the cave as a tear slowly trickled from her eyes fixed on eternity, which was opened to her.

Alberon froze when he saw the remains of the human on the ground. How did they get there? He stiffened as he realized.

"Lyra, you know our laws!"

Lyra, who was trying to decipher the inscriptions on the ceiling, turned and came down in a whirlwind of silvery light swirl. The whirlwind slowed down and condensed, giving way to a human form. Long, pale pink hair, dancing in the atmosphere by an invisible breeze, and widely spaced green eyes that stretched to the sides, Lyra was a different Daikini from the others. Born of a Daikini father and a human mother, she had inherited magic ... and beauty.

"No human has the right to enter the primitive temple except the priests! And at the invitation of the Sabians! It's sacred!

- The Sabians left it, and abandoned their fate to the humans.

- And they charged me, they charged us, with protecting the temple while awaiting their return. And thus you force me to forsake my contract!"

The Daikini people emerged from this torpor when they heard the clamor of their king. Each had his own color, projecting light onto the walls. Soon the room was filled with Daikinis.

All this took the form of a lawsuit by her own father, her own people, thought Lyra.

"A human and a baby, what a great threat indeed!" Lyra said, mocking with disapproval as the murmurs became silent.

"The body will be taken outside.

-      No!" Lyra screamed.

Alberon went to sit on top of Myrthe mirror. The Sabians had moved it with the tree. It had not been an easy task, since the mirror was embedded in the tree.

"It was I who betrayed you. It's true. I guided her.

- Why?

- Because she was wearing an Anjara medallion."

A silence fell. Then the whispers began again to rustle.

"What are you saying?

- Look for yourself, Father."

Alberon flew majestically and approached the remains of Morràn. The medallion was around the child's neck.

"I didn't bring them to the forest. But she was not far from the temple when I found her. I showed her the way, just to here.

- Was she followed?

- No Father. I closed the door after her."

Alberon thought intensely. The Anjara medallions were powerful talismans that had their own mind. They didn't just end up in the hands of anyone; nor did they just take them anywhere. Alberon dared not touch the remains.

"Only the Sages, the highest members of the caste of priests, and Sabians could enter the Temple. It is a sacred place ... we had the guard. My daughter Lyra broke that oath ... for a legitimate reason."

He was interrupted by a horn that sounded off in the plain. Onesimus, a friend of Lyra's childhood vanished in the air. He returned a few seconds later.

"The armed elves and their allies are massing troops on the plain, my King.

22

- Who are their allies? Lyra asked.

- Humans from the plains, the Begerri, the Loires, the Hounds, and magical creatures. That's not all. Some are amassed farther away. I do not know if the Tengu and the Sokars have joined the ranks of Goiri, I doubt it.

- Father, we must fight!

- My word, you have gone mad my daughter!

- Your Majesty, if all the creatures do not unite now, it will be too late. If we turn our backs, we run our loss.

- The humans have chosen their destiny! Their arrogance has brought them to this point!

- You are just as blind as they are! Someone maneuvered in the shadows: the man in black. No one had seen his true face, but everyone knew he has assembled these mercenaries to spread chaos. And today, the chaos spread around the corner. This is the man in black that surely leads the Sokars and Tengu. It's more than a force of good and evil at work outside.

- Indeed, we must make a decision: I must think of my people and their future."

Lyra felt reassured. Her father had finally understood.

"It will only take a few minutes to move the human army of the man in black, or of Faraoh to penetrate the forest Etheldrede and rampage.

- The priests have a plan, Father.

- What? Are you in contact with humans?

- No, I listened to them talk, just when they came to the Temple the last time.

- And what have they planned, these great minds, despite all that has happened?

- They will activate a shield to protect the forest.

- When?! Alberon screamed.

- I don't know ... "

Onesimus approached Lyra and materialized to take his hand. Alberon rose into the air and thundered:

"We have to go. Who knows what we'll find at our doors tomorrow. And we are not warriors.

- Father, no! "

Lyra couldn't believe it. They couldn't run away!

"You forced me do this, Lyra. We can't assume such a responsibility. Not our people. This war is not ours. We'll go to the Sabians, in their island, and wait for the shadows of this world to pass. We'll be safer there. Get ready, my daughter, for this great journey."

The king turned and went back into the palace hidden in the walls, but what he heard stopped him short:

"Farewell, Father," Lyra said sadly.

Lyra took the child in his arms, taking care of Morràn's remains. She heard only the whispers of ancient inscriptions that roamed the ceiling. She heard only the call of the medallion to take care of the child. Onesimus and her father screamed as she disappeared, the child with her. A Daikini could play with the wind and light. No could hold her back. No one could find her.

Chapter 3

He had been wrong to believe that he could defeat Faraoh. It had been too late for a long time. But hope was always nagging him. Aman paced the corridor. He waited for Wyre, who had left to look for novices, and Agaric, who was to return to the stairs after his interview with the Queen. He had given orders. The priests were to shave their beards, shed their uniforms for those of royal guards, or beggars, and to steer clear of Samatya. There was only one thing left to do. But the head of the council of Elders, the head of the Caste of priests, Aman couldn't help but doubt: he changed his mind. He wouldn't wait for Agaric, he would first alert Cassandra, who remained in the forest to activate the Azur. Etheldrede was a sanctuary where there were a lot of hidden creatures, and magic would be preserved through this magical shield. He went towards the common room where the fire was still burning in the fireplace. The army outside the Tengu and Sokars massacred the elf army and sacked Etheldredre to claim their territory. Soon, a red smoke filled the sky above Samatya.

Lyra reappeared behind the home of the priests. No one. She had to talk to them. She pressed the baby close to her, who was now playing with her hair. She was a beautiful little girl with green eyes. Strange— she could have sworn they were blue when she had seen them the first time. The infant looked at this wide-eyed creature bathed in light, with arms soft and fresh like a river. The noise of the battle tore Lyra's attention away from the baby. The blood flowed out. She felt it sting her flesh. The Daikinis didn't understand violence. It was something that came from humans. Not magic. There was no *Heka* in the act of slicing someone's throat. Suddenly, a red glow split the sky, and stagnated over the city, while Daikinis rose in the sky and sped south. Lyra had an idea. She had to take care of the human body which had been left in the Temple. The child would thank her later. She disappeared and rematerialized in the kitchen of the priests' home. She did not know who would come, but he would find no evil in this child, and they'd protect her. She ran her hand across the parchment where the child's name appeared, as she put the baby on the table, graciously wrapping her in cloth. The child drifted off to sleep, clutching the parchment. Perhaps it was intuition, or perhaps the medallion was speaking to her. She carefully grabbed the talisman off the child's neck.

Goiri, head of the royal guard riding majestically on his white stallion, was now blood-stained—he raised his sword and struck.

He would be able to relax just as soon as he sent these ungodly creatures back to where they came from: hell, with Iglal. These mercenaries and those fabulously trained robbers had become, in the space of a few months, professional killers. The magical creatures fell one after the other: Wildlife, Danaikvas who chose to ally with them, Leprechauns, changelings, Chimera, even Erythy were mobilized.

Goiri turned his gaze to the plain of Lyandre, his second son was to arrive with reinforcements of plains people, the Hounds and the Loires. The Royal Guard wasn't enough. Vaystran, his eldest, harangued the rearguard. With his sharp elf ears, he heard with pride:

"We must overcome the man in black! We have to prove to people and to the Queen, our loyalty. Our loyalty not to humans, but to the pact between all creatures of this world long ago. We must prove Faraoh is wrong. He manipulates the population, putting us in the same camp as the Tengu, the Sokars, and evil creatures. In defending this world, it's your life you are defending, but also the entire kingdom, your freedom, your future."

The troops roared ferociously, and fell forward, unaware of their lack of courage in the face of Faraoh's wave weapon.

The old abandoned mill dominated the hill and hid creatures from the eyes of others. Hiero was the highest of the Tengus; he was also the oldest. The army of Sokars, half reptile warriors who came from the mountain Ethil, and his own troops would sweep over the ridiculous army which fronted the mercenaries employed by the man in black. No one knew his face. Except him, Hiero. He had ripped off his mask. Not to kill him. But out of curiosity to see the true face of this man who had made a pact with the most evil races to sweep violence on the grounds of Hizaion. He bowed in respect to this man and his plan, which was simply brilliant. Hiero was shrouded in doubt by some of the Tengu. He clicked his tongue before spitting:

"I feel your doubts my brothers, my soldiers. The man in black infiltrated the city and we will soon open the doors. It was he who told us of the entrance to the underground, in the lands of Hizaion of the mill. It is he whom we gathered. We are on the verge of destroying the human swine as we have always dreamed of! Are you ready to feast yourself from these human dogs?"
Hiero screamed, tearing at the sky, brandishing a dagger. He preferred to deadlift his enemies and rip them in flight, but only Sokars meet the call of the sword. Bloodthirsty, thousands of Sokars and Tengu went up to the onslaught of what was left of the army of Goiri.

Cassandra had seen the signal of the Samatya temple and had cast lots; the signal, a red glow, was now above the temple in a threatening mass. She had left home, the foyer of the priests in the forest, running. She had to act quickly. Invoking the goddess, and taking the only horse before her, she left the edge of the wood and walked to the Twin Mountains. The stallion she rode then reared and spurred another direction: the plain where ferocious cries rang out. The priestess couldn't master the horse, it was as if he was driven by an invisible force. Coming to the exit of the forest, he didn't slow, but began jumping over bodies.

"Hevael! Just stop!"

She could not die on the battlefield! Her fate was different! It was necessary to activate the shield before ... Suddenly she saw Goiri on the ground, a part of his armor ripped off, his leg bloody. He held the body of his son Vaystran his arms, with a mad look on his face. Cassandra miraculously managed to stop the horse. If it is the will of the Goddess…cool and confident, she threw out a projection towards a Tengu that almost tore her face with her claws. The horrible creature flew off like a disjointed puppet. Insensitive to the smell of the dead, she charged Vaystran's body onto her mount, and helped Goiri to ride behind her. Hevael then returned himself and swept into the forest and the primitive temple. The battle was almost over, the corpses of elves piled up in the plain. It was a massacre perpetrated by the army of mercenaries and evil creatures who were paid by the man in black. Few survivors saw Cassandra spinning among the shining armor. They followed her, asking the goddess to forgive them their cowardice. There was no courage in dying anyhow. Especially when you were a magical creature. They were defeated. Hiero licked his teeth, landing gently on the plain, the time to gather his troops. It was time for the man in black to honor his promise. It was time to feast on Samatya ... Etheldrede and its magic would be the next step.

Trapped. They were trapped. Gathering the novices and the aspiring ones to the Caste had taken longer than expected, and the door was barricaded from the outside—they were trapped in the dormitory inside the temple. Faraoh had been alerted by the signal Aman had given to carry out his orders. The Sage couldn't use as much *Heka*, the vital energy to dematerialize as many individuals and rematerialize elsewhere. It was simply impossible. She was trying to locate Aman to call for help, but her mind was blurred. She cast a fire spell against the door, to no avail. Wyre tried to remain calm despite the novices who began to cry. Was it the weapon of Faraoh already in action?

Agaric was out of the Temple with a bang. Dressed in black as usual, no one had paid attention to this hairy man. No one would have taken him for a priest. He ran through the hall of the desert palace. All this was abnormal. Too quiet. Much too quiet. He heard loud voices coming from the right courtroom before him. He rushed recognizing the voice of the Queen.

"Reconciliation was still possible Faraoh! I cannot believe the betrayal of Goiri.

- My Queen, Goiri betrayed you. The pact sealed between all the magical races, and initiated by the Sabians is no more. They all want your throne. Moreover, it may make sacrifices to save something more important. Think of your girls. Power is a complex task, it depleted your husband.

- And you helped the snake there."

Surprised to see Agaric brave the danger to enter the throne room and confront him made him laugh. Faraoh was flattered by the last game with an opponent of the Caste ... before their extermination.

"What am I accused of exactly?

- I accuse you, Faraoh, of the King's murder, and to have masterminded the plot of his death.

- The King is dead from exhaustion, you heard his last words.

- I've never been able to examine his body. You came from out of the blue two years ago, and here you are next to the throne. You have everything installed, although I have no proof. I am convinced

32

that the man in black is your ally. I accuse you, as you accuse us, the honorable Caste of priests to persecute and despise the people of plotting conspiracies against the royal family.

- Did you honorably murder this girl tonight?

- It was an unfortunate accident committed by two idiots who were punished without trial.

- I can't control the crowd.

- I believe instead that you understand it perfectly."

Agaric, as wise as he was, could not stand anymore. He was going to project a *Heka* discharge on Faraoh, but he jumped towards the Queen and took out a dagger. Agaric held his hand radiating magic. Faraoh needed her, the population was still too attached to the royal family, he would not dare.

"Ho, Agaric, I'll risk it all."

And Faraoh sliced the throat of the Queen before his horrified eyes. The priest disappeared in a black smokescreen. He needed to save *Heka* to escape alive. Faraoh looked around quietly. It was not supposed to happen, but after all ... it would simplify the task. He slid the blade on the back of his hand and smeared blood on his forehead and brow bone. He then left the palace, staggering and opening the doors of the palace, he began to scream.

"The Queen was murdered by priests! Traitors! To me, the guard! The faithful!"

The soldiers he had himself sent on the walkway froze. Four of them rushed to the Temple. Faraoh fell to his knees and holding his head in his hands, began to moan in front of a few individuals that remained in public curiosity. An old man approached and tried to lift him up.

"Minister, only you can save us ...

- The task is immense ...

- And the princesses?"

Faraoh's eyes widened.

"You're right, I can still save them!"

Faraoh turned and ran.

Agaric was connected to Wyre, and had recovered. She greeted him with a desperate look.

"A man came and took the novices. I do not know where he took them ...»

Her lip was swollen.

"I didn't even cast a spell, he had a gun ...

- You mean ...

- Like the one who sits on the southwest tower."

Agaric raised his hand to the window, which was normally sealed. The lock sprang, and the two priests escaped by climbing the roof and diving into an alley.

34

A guard chased after them. Wyre grabbed Agaric by the hair and pushed her in front of him unceremoniously.

"Bitch, I'll teach you to want to rob me while I piss!"

The guard attempted a smirk towards Wyre and passed right by them. They sped to the north of the city.

Chapter 4

In his office, Faraoh closed his armoire quietly, thinking about what he would do with the novices. As a matter of fact, the princesses locked up in the west wing of the palace hadn't been able get out since last night. Time was a precious thing. It was the order he mastered the best. He took a plate of finely worked silver, emptying out a line of silvery liquid filled with tiny dancing crystals. Stealing the crystal fragment from the Sabians hadn't been easy. Vindhara was an outstanding guardian. More powerful than a magician, she had nevertheless made mistakes. This breed of Sabians had always been too proud. But he had to admit, their prophecies were very useful to him. He was convinced he was the Destroyer, day after day. He was born into nothing, and he was now the highest among the Sabians—and one day, he would allow the world to rid itself of them. He didn't hate magic, contrary to what the priests said: but magic must be controlled by someone who deserves it, and for the service of progress. The Sabians had transmitted crumbs of this knowledge to humans, but they had let them live in the mire for decades.

"As a seed yields a tree that will one day fall to ashes, we must respect humans' rhythms," his mentor had told him.

So much naivety in such a wise person... but it was not wisdom that guided the world. Faraoh had understood. He was even smarter than Sabians themselves, who hadn't seen the viper amongst them, feeding off of their knowledge.

He glanced at the quartz dial on the wall. It was a marvel of technology that was impossible to find in the Hizaion lands. It was this kind of instrument that had amazed the King and his court, crumbling it to pieces and earning his trust. It would bring the city, and then the land, to a level of science that nobody had ever seen. Not even the Sabians. When he'd finished with him, he would take care of the novices. Agaric had probably taken Wyre with him. Regardless, their resistance was already broken before being born.

He turned and threw a balled up rag to the chained to the man before him, who had been brought to his knees.

"If you defeat me in this duel, you'll be pardoned. Here," he said, as he unchained him. "Put these clothes on. Now, if you succeed, you'll join the militia that protects the population."

The man, whose face was haggard, didn't take his eyes from the black garment in his hand. It was his only chance.

"Assault weapons are on the wall. Chose one. Any. Defend your life."

The man with the weathered face and calloused hands dressed awkwardly. Faraoh clicked his tongue in annoyance and straightened out the clothes of the man he'd brought from prison. He pulled down the hood that had completely covered his face.

"Ah, now don't you look great!" He remarked, slamming his hand on his shoulder.

Erynée had obeyed the minister. He was the man of the hour. For years now, he'd maintained unity in the country. The royal family, one may say, was completely overwhelmed by the situation. But they were still a sacred symbol for the kingdom. They had been in power for generations. If the two princesses disappeared ... the old woman shuddered. What would become of them? She'd hidden under the bridge, listening to the battle raging outside, unable to distinguish the orders. If only she could get on the walkway. It was forbidden and dangerous. Only the militia had access. It was protected by Faroah's personal guard and driven by his whims. They had been put in the service for the city by the royal family a few months ago, ever since the guard of Goiri had deserted. People emerged, driven by curiosity, and were gathered on the walkway. The cries of the Tengu and Chimera tore the sky. Suddenly, on the balcony of the royal palace not far from the Temple, Faraoh fought. He was fighting with the man in black!

It had gone on long enough: the duel began in his office. The strapping man had thrown him against the window, causing it to shatter. They had an audience, and the final scene was about to take place. He didn't have the same sturdier build of his opponent and his sword was becoming heavier. He parried a shot, kicked his opponent in the back, and pulled out his weapon, the same he had equipped his personal militia with. He pointed it at the man in black. He began screaming, while the weapon waving about in the hands of Faraoh continued to burn the human flesh through its steel point. After a few seconds of horrible contortions, the man stopped moving. There was silence, heavier than ever. The minister then waved his gun at the sky and harangued the crowd:

"People of Hizaion, the man in black is dead! Punished by the science I created! The army of foul creatures is defeated, and we must continue to cleanse the land for a new era! "

Faraoh rolled up the body of the unfortunate man: it went crashing down the steps of the palace. The crowd chanted:

"The prophecy! He must burn! Burn him!"

They seized the remains and threw the body on the steps of the temple with all the wood they could gather: paintings, sculptures, bowls, and utensils. They set fire and screaming with joy, looked at it with fascination, as the flames blazed the temple. Erynée chanted Faraoh's name with the others. Yes, he was the man of the hour.

With a gesture, Faraoh ordered the weapon to be brought to the outside, where it was swiveled around. All the magical creatures would be annihilated.

A muffled sound, faint at first, grew persistently. The army of Tengu and Sokars stopped short. Those who were in flight fell to the ground, breaking their winged formation. The Sokars retreated swiftly, while spitting and disappearing over the horizon in only a few minutes, while waving their reptile tails. Hiero, ears bloodied, roared. His warriors died at his feet, betrayed by Faraoh. Rendered mute by hatred, he gritted his teeth and swore silently, heading towards Etheldrede.

With resolution, Cassandra opened the door and slipped down the stairs that Morràn hadn't seen the day before. There, deep in the land of Hizaion, the priestess had safely reached the room she was searching for: a stone altar with finely braided grooves, a true work of art. A beautifully carved crystal icicle hung from the ceiling. Chanting prayers for the opening of the ritual, Cassandra lowered the two bodies she had made to levitate drop gently to the ground. Their eternal rest in these places had been decided by the goddess herself. Even though her plans sometimes eluded her, she always bowed to them. After all, they came from the royal line. Quick! She grabbed the sword supported by two statues of a Sabian and a priest, and slid the tip into the in the almost invisible slot, overhung by crystal.

"Arrach naha zar!"

Her voice vibrated in the air, as she powerfully took the hilt of the sword. The crystal emitted a blast that shook the walls, and reached Samatya through the air, activating the Azur. The palace windows exploded while the crowd dispersed screaming, believing that the priests had a secret weapon. Erynée covered her head in her hands like the others, in a pitiful reflex to protect the sky from falling on them. She ran into the streets to hide at home. Faraoh watched his plan turn to ashes, and he screamed with rage: blinding light shot out of the pyramid, and formed a perfect sphere of light around the forest. The shield that protected Etheldrede and its past relics was activated, encompassing the forest.

Cassandra approached Goiri, who lay dying: the wounds were deep, and he had lost too much blood. As she suspected, he would die. She lay him on her, resting him on her chest.

"The reinforcements never came. Samatya, the land of Hizaion, is lost.

- Goiri, calm yourself."

The noble traits of the warrior tensed, seeing Vaystran resting nearby.

"My son ... my ..."

Goiri's eyes widened and he grabbed her hand.

"My son will return."

Cassandra kissed him on the forehead as he drew a final breath. *"He was never king. But he could have been a fine one,"* seemed to say the face of Dana, carved in a faraway smile.

Aman waited in front of the foyer: he had to know exactly how many had escaped. His mind was clouded by Faraoh's weapon. What power ... capable of disrupting the *Heka* of an elder Sage. He thoughtfully sat down on a stone. It wasn't but noon, but they had to organize the resistance. His death was nothing compared to the extinction of all these magical breeds Faraoh had destroyed this morning. Aygulf, Ferens, and a dozen other priests and priestesses appeared.

"The good thing is that the *Yatras* will be easier now that the crystal is activated. Crystal pieces are valuable for making teleportation trips, and only members of the Council possess them. Except of course Cassandra, if she needs to contact us ... But ... Where are the novices?"

Wyre and Agaric appeared in a burst of light, clinging to each other.

"Aman, the Queen has been assassinated by Faraoh!

- The novices ... he took them from me.

- Aman, what do you think he'll do with them?"

Dared to ask Ferens.

The Sage stood and watched their faces tense ahead.

"It will depend on the crowd. Either he will use them as an example to eradicate magic once and for all, or he will kill them by militia and accuse us of human sacrifice ... We can no longer do anything for Samatya. But we can find other novices, and continue our work ... at Rosendal."

Their faces stooped, disappointed.

"Faraoh doesn't have a long enough arm to reach us there."

Wyre advised Fauns and Leprechauns who staggered through the trees.

And what about them?

- They're safe here.

- One of us should stay here to help Cassandra.

- No. We must organize the resistance. I have every confidence that Cassandra will fulfill her mission. She accepted. She's now the guardian of the forest and its magic now that the Azur has been activated. Don't lose hope."

The entire Caste approached Aman as he brought forth a translucent crystal fragment as thick as a fist. He waved it toward the sky: a blinding flash enveloped them, and they disappeared.

Lyra passed through the walls, dematerializing her body through the quartz rooms and amethyst hallways, like a ghostly apparition. What would become of their beautiful palace? They'd occupied it since the departure of the Sabian people, the founders of the kingdom of Hizaion. It was their inheritance, their home, their heavenly realm embellished over generations. All these wonders of civilization could suddenly collapse, as the world was an unknown road ... The opal mirror crimped and ruffled as crystals and falling stalactites reflected the evanescent silhouette of the Daikini's different angles. Sometimes the mirror reflected a face with tender sketches, fine and soft features, crowned with pink hair floating in the air. Sometimes it showed a cluster of bright dust, or a crazy arabesque spiral winding sensually. Lyra was Daikini made of wind and water. She used both elements perfectly to blend in or stand out. She was now alone in the room of the Myrthe mirror, which through a bluish glow on the floor shone its frame. Who was this woman, the mother of the child? Broad forehead, high cheekbones, an aquiline nose, thin lines ... How had she managed to get an Anjara medallion? On the other side of the world, she felt an unusual soul, who had succumbed to death in its own way.

"Be at peace, the gods have heard you." She said, closing the Morràn's eyelids.

Clasping her hands over her body, she blew three times on her heart, her mouth, and her eyes.

A frost was forming on her clothing, and soon, under the hand of Lyra, the body was wrapped in a thin silver dust. Under the haunting voice of Daikini, which penetrated every wave of air, the cocoon crystallized. Yet, Lyra was struggling. It was harder than she thought. She would have to give more vital energy to the form a shrouded envelope to protect the body. Lyra thought of Andraste. She didn't even know her mother ... *If only Onesimus had been there* ... but she didn't have a choice. Lyra then closed her eyes and gave all the *Heka* she could. She wouldn't be able to take care of the child immediately as she'd hoped. She would wait for the forest to regenerate for a few years until Andraste grew and was ready to receive her inheritance.

Cassandra was shocked when she discovered the child. She fed her goat's milk she had on hand, rocked her, and examined her. The clothes she was swaddled in were incredibly fine.

"Andraste ... why and how did you come to me," questioned the priestess.

Sitting in the chair, she let the child play with her hair. She had fiery red hair that she had taken down from a braid. She looked at the two hourglasses she'd turned over. One indicated the time outside, the other within the Azur. The day finished here while only an hour had scarcely elapsed since Faraoh had screamed with rage. Suddenly she froze: the child clutched in his hands the selenite fragment the priestess always kept around her neck. It cracked.

"But..." Cassandra gasped in surprise.

The perfume of twilight mingled with the fog, and rolling trees on the hills in the distance, as everything was a blur of confusion in the mind of the forest's new guardian.

Chapter 5

The sky was torn in half and emptied itself onto the earth. Andraste closed her eyes with delight. The clouds were so dark that one couldn't tell whether it was night or dawn. It was her favorite time. Her agile mind took over, *"Will it also rain in the city, the world of oblivion?"*

The rain began to beat the thatched roof, and ran into the gutters from the garden, washing away the sins of the land of Hizaion. The air crackled in the lightning that struck the ground, and the rain became so thin that the wind swept and convoluted it. The god Ethil rumbled of an unquenched thirst. It had been sixteen years since the war was over inside the Azur. Andraste saw all this, or guessed it, through the crack in the door. She heard Cassandra's frame creak and leapt up. Aspiring to join the Caste required obedience, but only the one who showed inner discipline could reach the level of Sage someday. Andraste dreamed of reaching the summits.

Clouds escaped and light poured out of the heavens, giving way to the gods in the forest of Etheldrede, the sanctuary protected by a powerful spell that kept them from the world of oblivion.

She jumped out of bed, and began to comb her hair: three braids on the side tied with a yellow ribbon. It was the traditional hairstyle of the novices. She wore brown burlap pants, an olive-colored linen shirt, and a dark brown homespun jacket, made from an old coat of a priest who had left it there. Cassandra sighed.

"It's not the traditional dress, but novices only come to the forest for the initiation ceremony in which they become apprentices."

Andraste sometimes secretly went into the back room and caressed the traditional clothing. One day, it would be hers.

She looked in the mirror: a pale face, with big blue eyes and dancing reflections, and blond hair which looked much darker in winter, when the sun of Oryon became rarer. My, she looked quite nice.

In a few hours, she would be on the highest branch of her favorite tree near the river. She would watch the horizon hidden by the Azur smoke, the invisible barrier protecting Etheldrede. But in the meantime, she would perform her daily chores composed of cleaning their foyer. The goal was to be ready for the Sages at any time. Andraste came and went in the forest, but never straying too far away. The forest was a territory itself within the Hizaion lands that belonged to the gods and priests, and the young novice had not yet explored it.

They worked all morning, in silence. Cassandra, who didn't lose her luster even dressed like a peasant, loved the silence: the land taught them patience and humility. How many lice infested beans had she harvested the first year! She'd used a spell to protect the early shoots, snails, and other small creatures, otherwise they would have died of hunger.

48

At noon, the sun shone to reward them for their efforts. When Cassandra pushed open the kitchen door, Andraste had prepared the stew: it was the traditional meal for when the days became cooler. Spinach, carrots and almonds, with bread. The bread was the most difficult thing to do. Fortunately, Etheldrede had foreseen everything, anticipating the dark events that ended with the Battle of Goiri. A wheat plain stretched not far from home. Harvesting, sorting, and grinding the wheat was the most physical work.

"Dana, mother of all things born of the earth, Aum, the father of all things descended from heaven, thank you for this meal. Love and light to all magical beings and magic of these lands. May your magic always burn and may your magic return."

The last two sentences were not part of the prayer, but Cassandra had agreed to add them. In the mouth of a child, the healer and guardian of the forest found the prayer particularly moving.

The leaves rustled in the wind that drove the clouds. Their orange reflections mingled with Andraste's curls.

"A party. We'll have a party for your birthday!"

The girl couldn't believe her ears.

"Well, the weather is exceptional today, so yes, we will have a ball. It always rains on the day of your birthday, but the wind is with us today. We'll put on nice clothes, a big fire, and I'll conjure a few pieces of wood to play music and we'll dance! Sixteen years old, that's something to celebrate!"

"There's no more far-away Prince to seduce so why bother," Andraste sighed inwardly.

"You don't need a prince to have a party," laughed Cassandra.

"And anyway, belonging to the Caste of priests means respecting chastity."

Andraste hated when she used her powers on her. She felt naked and vulnerable when Cassandra caught her thoughts on the fly. She could sometimes protect her mind by imagining a door in front of her, but it was tiring to always be on guard.

She never took naps, but she still climbed into the tree that dominated their clearing: a large oak tree at the high branches which hosted the lessons of Andraste. She now knew by heart the tale land of Hizaion and its wisdom, the country's history, and the Caste. In recent years, Cassandra taught her spells to control *Heka* at an exceptionally high level for a novice. Every day, Cassandra saw her protégé grow more and more; she would be a member of the Council of Sages someday. Probably before her twenty-fifth birthday. But she had to wait until the initiation ceremony to teach her all she knew. The novitiate was mostly a series of trials to test the level of *Heka* of the novice, to learn discipline, and to shape their minds. Cassandra nursed the hope that Aman himself could take guardianship to accelerate her training. Such an element in the Caste was welcome in these troubled times, she thought, observing Andraste levitating dead leaves by their stems. The guardian of the forest blessed every day since she had found the child at the foyer. But if she had had the choice, would she have agreed to join the Caste? Even she was only five years old when Aygulf had come for.

"Do we belong to the Caste forever?"

The novice surprised the magician with her reflections:

"Yes. Some have denied the Caste and become wanderers. We turn away from the Caste by cowardice or a thirst for power. I hope that you will choose the right path." She said harshly.

"Being of service to others is a difficult path. But this is our mission, Andraste.

- It's just... turning sixteen, it makes me think. I don't realize what I learn because I'm all alone here. I mean, I feel that everything is going so slowly. I have no novice friend to exchange with or to talk about my progress with. I feel so lonely."

And that was the truth. Andraste felt more alone than ever. Abandoned in this world, following a tortuous path of suffering. Cassandra took her hand.

"Look."

She had put an inanimate beetle in her palm. Looking closer, it was a scarab carved in a labradorite stone of power. And when Cassandra muttered an inaudible spell for the novice, the scarab became animated.

"Magic takes time. Like art, like land. Patience and time. That is why the time slows down in Etheldrede. It is a blessing."

Andraste watched, fascinated by the beetle flying slowly before their eyes. Cassandra waved her palm and contracted her eyes and fingers, gripping the creature, forcing it to fly.

"Going against this rate is destructive."

To the left, to the right, above…the creature gesticulated, distraught. Andraste worried for the small creature but didn't dare interrupt the magician during her demonstration. Cassandra dropped her hand and put the beetle in Andraste's palm. The priestess passed the palm of her hand over the beetle, causing it to become lifeless. Cassandra could be hard. Harsh and unforgiving.

"Did you see how I gave it magic? Then emptied the magic afterwards?

- Yes…

- It's called a relic. The magic was extracted, and the object became useless.

- Can I keep it?

- If you like." Cassandra said nonchalantly. She stood up and clapped her hands: Come on! Go fetch wood. Don't go beyond the river, and if it is too heavy, levitate it!

- Yes, Cassandra."

Andraste left. She thought she saw a light there before her. She followed it, and before she realized it, she found herself in front of the milky-looking wall. She tried to close her mind so her thoughts couldn't be read. She'd be punished for going over the river, and for approaching the Azur.

"Power is nothing bad. The thirst for power and the belief that you are the equivalent of a god is what corrupts the hearts and minds, Andraste," she heard.

Who's there?!" Screamed the novice.

She had nothing to defend herself with. Not even a magic wand to project spells. Then the wind blew, shaking the trees behind it. A flock of tiny birds flew perfectly coordinated. The light reappeared before her:

"Remember the wind in your hair when you slept in your tree. Remember playing with butterflies when you were a child. Remember the music when you looked at yourself in the reflection of the sparkling water."

Andraste did remember: a presence that had accompanied her from childhood, invisible but playful and loving. She had believed in fairies, but this was something else. The light became more aggressive to her eyes, and suddenly, Lyra was there. Her long pink hair, her eyes laughing and arms floating in the air, light and playful.

"Forty years have passed outside since you were born.

- But ... Who are you?

- I was at your birth, and I brought you to the guardian of the forest.

- But ... why didn't you keep me? You ... You didn't want me when I was born?

- Oh no! Don't think that, Andraste! On the contrary! But I had to do something for your mother... And I became too weak."

The sensation of Lyra's hands on her arms was strange: fresh, like a breeze, or a tickle.

"I am a Daikini. The last of the forest. The rest left Etheldrede the day of the battle for the Sabian Goiri country.

- Ha ... Cassandra didn't find you, that's what she thinks.

- Are you happy with her?

- Yes I am. She teaches me little by little, but ... Well, Lyra, where is my mother? I need to see her.

- Andraste, your mother died. I'm sorry."

The novice bowed her head sadly.

"Your father most likely as well.

- Who was he?

- I don't know. A member of the guard I presume. He had to have died in battle. Your mother came from Samatya, that, I'm sure. She was dressed humbly, but she had courage. I think she was someone noble. None were spared by the acts of Faraoh, which favored the little people, you know."

Andraste was troubled. She threw caution to the wind.

"Do you want to learn Andraste?

- Oh yes!

- Why?

- Well ... I'm not satisfied being just a novice. I want ... I want more.

- You want to learn because magic is the only thing you firmly know. You're filled with it, I feel it. You know that. And Etheldrede is your family."

Lyra said softly.

"Teach me Lyra. Take me with you!"

Lyra elegantly raised her hand and a leaf rose. She spoke softly, swirling it for a few moments. Andraste was fascinated. Then the leaf was kindled, but instead of being reduced to ashes, it continued to burn, like a wick. Then the flames ceased, and Andraste, eyes wide in surprise, saw a pearl of dew in the heart of the leaf. And it again became green and tender.

"Life comes from *Heka*, the invisible substance of which we are made. And magic is the art of playing with this material. But it's a big responsibility.

- Cassandra taught me the meaning of the colors and how to dedicate a candle a few days ago.

- I see."

The healer probably had her reasons to slow the training of the child. But the world of oblivion hadn't forgotten them! Faraoh wouldn't give up his plans. And the time elapsing within the Azur was to be put to use.

"It's my birthday today.

- I know. I will offer you many gifts.

- Oh yes?

- Yes. Gifts that give you power. The power to change things."

The girl shuddered. She took a look into the world of oblivion, a blur behind the magic shield.

"You will return to it. You come from this world. And there you will have all the answers you seek."

The novice would have liked the Daikini to come to party, but Lyra preferred to decline. She wanted to observe from afar the behavior of the guardian. If she approached, the healer would feel it, so it was necessary that she be measured in her contacts with

Andraste.

Lyra watched as she disappeared to fetch wood under the seal of the elms that lined the forest. Yes, she was filled with magic, much more than a human should be. The Council of Sages would have its most powerful member if they agreed to continue her training. She stood there, standing beside the being that could tip the scales in their favor and restore magic in this world.

Andraste, pensive, suddenly had an idea while walking on the trail. The Longuins lived in this part of the forest. Perhaps had they musical instruments? That's when the attack occurred. Everything happened at the speed of lightning. A half human creature with messy black hair jumped on her back, gripping her throat. Lyra's name couldn't even cross her lips.

"Your blood spills blood!" Yelled the Dagyde.

With rage, the novice grasped the creature by her hair, and tore it off of her. Her assailant screamed in pain and let go. Andraste rushed to a piece of wood and stone while her enemy was scraping the ground with her nails through gritted teeth.

"My word, you fight like a real girl!" Sneered the young girl.

A dazzling flash appeared, and Lyra intervened. The Dagyde cowered on the ground, moaning.

Who are you? Lyra asked.

- Created by the Red Witch. Created to kill and only to kill.

- You were part of the troops of Faraoh, weren't you? Created to battle Goiri?"

The Dagyde nodded. She was a miserable creature with black mop of tangled hair, and a body rolled into strips. Her white skin was marked with notches and symbols in black ink. Andraste could only feel pity for her. But the Daikini continued:

You lie. Red Witches have all disappeared. Hizaion exterminated them long ago."

The Dagyde passed an earthy tongue over her lips as if she wanted to crucify the novice.

"One remains. One lives. Trust betrayed. Unholy blood."

The Daikini made a gesture that silenced her and stared in her eyes. The Dagyde couldn't handle the look, and the pure light of Daikini. She hooted like an owl, and fled among the foliage.

"Don't worry. She's fled to the Twin Mountains, Indra and Bashat. You won't cross her again.

- How...

- She must have left the battlefield and slipped into the forest before the Azur fell.

- How does one kill a Dagyde?

- Never used magic to kill or injure a living thing, magical or not. You hear me Andraste? Never.

- Why? She's the one that attacked me!

- You'd be cursed. Like Red Witches."

At these words, the girl was silent and looked at the stone in her hand. Lyra asked gently:

"Cassandra asked you to collect firewood. Think of the party tonight. The creature won't return, I promise."

Andraste spent the next hour piling wood, left alone by Lyra. But it was the levitation of wood to the foyer that took the longest. Concentrating her mind while watching where she set foot was a daunting task. Especially when she felt like she was being watched. Was it the Longuins? She had completely forgotten!

It was a wonderful evening that dispelled the grief of Andraste's doubts. When she arrived, Cassandra had prepared the most delicious meals, and a small firework show. In a few rounds of wrist twirls and murmurs, branches became animated drums and flutes. Andraste even thought she saw fades, little fairies becoming too scarce, dancing in the forests. They danced around the fire, laughing, as the branches changed pace, forcing them to change their moves.

Then the night became calm. The dying fire crackled as the two women sat laughing on a tree trunk in the clearing. After a pause, the girl asked the question that was burning her lips since the incident.

"Are there still Red Witches?"

Cassandra froze.

"Why are you asking me this?"

Andraste then visualized the image of the Dagyde leaping forward, taking care to remove Lyra from his mind. Cassandra widened her eyes.

"I was tackled this afternoon by a Dagyde that claims to accomplish revenge against Faraoh by a Red Witch. I don't understand."

Cassandra put her hands on her temples and stared at the ground, speechless. Andraste was frightened.

"Cassandra, how is this possible?

- Yes there is a Red Witch. Because she helped Faraoh in his quest for power. This is the genius of this evil being: he uses magic against ourselves. A weapon that we had forgotten. But I didn't think she was still living...

- Why would she seek revenge for Faraoh?

- He betrayed her as he betrayed his supporters to his reign alone. He wouldn't share power.

- But ... How she was able to escape the Caste?

- Because I helped her."

Andraste widened her eyes, her throat dry.

"I helped her because she's my sister."

The novice was speechless.

"I could have stopped her at Rosendal. She wanted so much to learn magic, like me. But she was rejected at the time when Aygulf came and chose me to join the Caste. She decided to learn the other magic. Dark magic. Red magic. That of Aradia. She officiated in the Rosendal Mountains where she practiced rites. I could've denounced her."

Andraste came and took her hands.

"I'll keep your secret."

But the magician gently pushed her away, turning her head.

"No need. Any Caste member knows."

Andraste was silent before this revelation. Why had she not been banned?

"Staying here locked up for decades without talking to anyone is not a reward, my dear."

She took her face in her hands.

"Fortunately you came. You were the light from the first day in that dark tunnel."

But she stiffened, almost regretting her gesture of affection and patting her on the shoulder, and got up to return to the foyer.

"Being part of the Caste is an honor. I hope you follow the steps and when the time comes to move on to the next step, you'll be ready and worthy."

Andraste nodded silently. The festival ended on a sour note.

"Starting tomorrow we begin the teachings of the last year of the novitiate. Sleep well, Andraste."

Chapter 6

"You will choose a tree in Etheldrede to make your wand.

- From the whole forest?

- Yes. But I advise you not to go too far. You have two days. Here's an amulet that will protect you."

Cassandra bent over to tie the cord behind the girl's neck. It was a piece of blue stone encased in a silver mount.

"Is it a crystal?

- Don't touch it!"

Andraste looked taken aback. Why had she cried out? Her guardian never yelled at her.

"I ... it's very fragile. That is why it's protected by the frame."

Cassandra arranged it on her coat, so it didn't touch her skin.

There you go. It'll create a shield, and will keep your assailant away.

-Is the forest of Etheldrede dangerous?

- You've always stayed close to home where no magical creature ventured. After the mishap with your Dagyde, I cannot let you go unprotected. Other creatures may lurk. I can locate you with this pendant."

Andraste strolled and often stopped to eat a bit of bread. It was autumn, making the trees blaze in a symphony of shimmering colors. It was her favorite time of the year. She plunged into the forest to the west, taking care to keep the two Twin Mountains on the left, in her sights. Andraste was not convinced of Cassandra's talisman of protection and feared coming face to face with the Dagyde.

Then she saw it. It was like a dream. A clearing full of sun where a huge Yew stood, branches circling around in the wind. The twisted trunk was hollow, like a coffin, and huge Yew stood majestically, stretching its biting leaves to the sky in all its glory. Andraste ran to the tree and touched the trunk. It was a wonderful feeling. She could feel the sap, weak, because it was the fall, but present.

"It's odd that you've chosen this tree."

Lyra came to rest on a high branch.

"This is a Yew. No other tree can grow next to it, I know!

- Certainly. But there are only a few Yews in the land of Hizaion. And the closest is the one that dominates the plain before Samatya.

- Oh really? But where do they come from?

- The gods planted them there. Iglal, the god of the underworld, holds one in his kingdom. And Manda, the sacred tree of the

Sabians is one too. These are like reproductions of the same element, like a mirror to infinity.

- The Iglal tree produces apples that give you eternal life.

- That's right, yes."

Andraste began to climb the branches one by one. When she reached the top, she gasped at the sight. She had never seen the magic shield in its entirety, from one end to the other of the horizon. It vibrated the light and became incandescent. There, in the distance, Samatya stood, like a mirage.

"Lyra ... could it be that you made a mistake? I mean ... My parents may still be alive.

- I attended your birth, Andraste. Your mother was on the other side."

The girl lowered her head sadly, her throat tightening. She looked at the foyer and saw no smoke. Strange... Cassandra had let the heat of the fire go out.

"I have something to show you. Come along with me."

Andraste grabbed a branch thanking the tree for its gift, and broke it before descending to follow the Daikini.

Cassandra was leaning on the table, looking at a map. Fortunately, she had everything down from that night: the date and approximate time of the birth of Andraste. Sixteen years had passed within the Azur... She was watching the position of planets on the astronomical map, a frown on her beautiful face: she had drawn tracks, red dots, lines and matches. She stood up, rubbing her lower back. The diagram showing the different stars in the sky present at the child's birth was complicated. Very complex. She had looked at this map several times to probe its fate: did she have the qualities needed to belong to the religious caste? Today she wanted to look with new eyes.

Andraste was born in solar house V of the Chimera and Lunar house II of Sokar, upward of Pyrauste. Two opposite signs. Fire and water. Light and darkness. Bravery and transformation: the two signs and the ascendancy showed a need to live intensely. A peaceful life is not enough for her, doubt would play quite a role. She had written in her the desire to change things and people, and especially a spirit of sacrifice. Sothya, the moon and the sun, Oryon were in balance within her: Sothya held back the tide and gave the momentum to make decisions, while Oryon gave her impatience and passion to bet on the future.

Cassandra rolled up the map and put it away on the top shelf: how far could she guide her, push her? The child had shown certain qualities growing up that were undeniable curiosity: involvement and a certain idealism—but it was time to seek advice from Aygulf, her old mentor.

64

The magician moved and fell motionless for a *Yatra*, a trip she hadn't done in a long time. Resting her hands on both sides of the chair by the hearth, her breathing became slow and inaudible.

The ancient towers stood in the blue, impassible and beautiful. The black slate shone and dazzled Cassandra. She looked around the tower where her colleagues were to be in full council. A noise. She stopped in the doorstep. The hallways smelled of desert and sulfur. The walls oozed suffering. She could feel it. No, it was blood. She heard complaints, screaming, the invasion of the corridors resonated in the walls. It was awful. She went back in her head in order to get away. Suddenly, someone pulled her back. The presence led her across the stairs to the top. They passed through the walls, while parading in the head of Cassandra, dazed. Suddenly, the presence let go and she felt the hard, cold marble against her cheek.

The presence was not threatening. Cassandra looked around. It was a room that was unknown to her. A tired voice spoke to her then, emerging from the darkness:

"My dear, you haven't changed ..."

Cassandra looked up and saw Aygulf, her former tutor.

"Aygulf! How happy I am to see you!"

They embraced warmly.

"Cassandra, astral travel is dangerous. What are you doing here?

- Where is the bird of ill omen?

- Ferens? Out in the forest. He's giving the children of Rosendal a class today.

- You've started classes? So you're looking for novices?

- We try Cassandra ... It's very complicated.

- Aygulf, I wonder about the child I collected sixteen years ago. I need to know what I can teach her."

Aygulf came and took her hand, covering it with his warm and reassuring palm.

"It is true that the training is not in your mission, but why don't you respect the program? I mean, you yourself were trained by me.

- It's just ... Aygulf. She's really talented. I mean ... I've never seen so much *Heka* in a human being."

The venerable priest muttered under his breath and went to the window looking at the red roofs of the city of Rosendal. The Gulf of Rosendal with its soft and glassy sea was caressed by the sun. There was a long table with books, scrolls, and feathers. Aygulf was an isolated priest, but studious. He occupied this part of the former University of Rosendal along with Ferens. They hid in truth, leaving the rest of the abandoned buildings to avoid attracting attention.

Cassandra had risen and was approaching the table. There were many books, but also a few plant-filled jars. Some minerals were placed on the table in the center, and the light came shimmer the finest stone of all, the most majestic, and the most noble: a crystal fragment, the quartz.

"I thought that protecting the city of Rosendal, this pearl of the south, would be easier. But we are the only two here: Ferens and I hiding like rats, helping people as we can. We didn't have enough crystal to create a protective sphere around the city and surrounding areas ... Even the city of Granada doesn't have any priests ... The Sabians jumped ship.

- What are you doing with the crystal?

- I'm trying to contact Vindhara ... They have no priests, no crystals, but they have more than that. Then, they welcomed Daikinis. Who knows, maybe they welcomed other races of the ancient world. Maybe that resistance isn't broken.

- Yes. Aygulf, we truly have a hope. Her name is Andraste. She is smart, fast, enduring.

- We are a Council of Sages, and some priests are even helpless facing the militia and Faraoh. What could a child contribute?

- She's not just a child ... I see it every day. She knows things intuitively, including things beyond her age, and her human condition. It is true that she adopts the way I live, and I have to explain some things, sometimes they're hard for her to accept.

- An anarchist seed!

- We're already in anarchy, Aygulf."

The old priest scratched his beard with his immaculate nails and remained silent for a moment. He turned his ring, a symbol of his rank in the caste, staring at the worm-eaten wood of the window.

"Tell me about her.

- Well, she shows certain skills for combat. She likes it. She has so much energy already. She radiates *Heka.* My crystal fragment couldn't even resist when she was a newborn.

- What do you mean?

- I mean it cracked from the inside on contact."

Aygulf stiffened.

"How old did you tell me she was?

- Sixteen years in our forest.

- I mean ... When was she born?

- In the fall, about forty years ago ... for you ... The day of the Battle of Goiri.

- How did she get in the forest?

- I don't know. When I returned the original temple, someone had placed her inside."

68

The priest kept silent, facing the window.

"Aygulf, I understand your concern about ... some abnormalities. But I cannot understand your suspicion: the key to resistance is at hand!"

The old priest looked serious, and asked:

"Do you know the prophecies of the Sabians, Cassandra? I mean *the* prophecy of which we thought was Faraoh the object.

- I... I know what the Council of Sages left us: *Born shall be a child who will seal the Iron Age, Temple destroyed magic returned. While man hesitates to conquer the dawn, the Destroyer will rise, and all the stars will fight among them. The Comet, sign of the storm, will announce the light of Ashera.*

- What if the Destroyer wasn't Faraoh?"

Lyra stood basking on top of a rock. Her pink hair danced in the shape of a corolla.

"Cassandra doesn't teach you because you're a novice. That is why they lost the last battle. They are entangled in their own obsolete honor code. But the war is not over, Andraste.

- Isn't Andraste a powerful goddess?

- Yes.

- Have you met her?

- No, silly!"

The Daikini laughed a crystalline laugh.

"Nobody meets the gods! They are in the other world. Hell or Gwenethil, the underworld or the white world.

- What hasn't Cassandra taught me?

- She will teach you many things, myself as well. But know something. You can create your own forms, your own rituals. It takes a high level of *Heka* and a perfect mastery of one's emotions. You should also give up some other powers, because you can't have everything.

- What skills should be abandoned?

- Telepathy, duplication, materialization ... they're probably the most difficult.

- So we can't be all powerful?

- No Andraste. Life is full of choices and sacrifices. Renunciations.

- What did you sacrifice, Lyra?"

Lyra replied with a soft smile. They arrived in a clearing, formerly well maintained, lined with pebbles half buried in the earth. There were a few flat stones of volcanic origin, some flat on the ground, others stuck in the grass as attested shelves of a former place of worship. In front of her was erected a small pyramid, half covered by leaves and roots, with a door carved on the facade. Andraste heard herself exclaim aloud:

70

"The first temple..."

The novice shuddered when entering the vast circular, dark room. Lyra opened the door to the room of Myrthe the mirror.

"We, the people of Daikinis loved this place very much, it was our palace many years ago

- What happened here?

- You. You were born here, Andraste."

Lyra then lit the back of the temple. On the ground lay an inanimate form, wrapped in a white shroud. Andraste trembled, her heart pounding. She dared not to try and understand what she was seeing. She knelt down and looked at the woman wrapped in a delicate matter: floating on chrysalis or snow crystals, it was hard to say...

"Is that...

- Your mother."

Andraste was in shock. She couldn't take her eyes away from her face. What color were her eyes? Was she the same? Did she have the same laugh?

"Who was she? How ... did she live in the forest?

- No. She went into the forest the night before the battle, protected by an Anjara medallion. It was around her neck. Take it, it is up to you. This is your inheritance."

Andraste put out her hand and noticed that she was trembling. Yet she was not afraid.

"I guided her, so she could enjoy the full power of this sacred place. We are just over a vortex of *Heka*. But once she gave you life, it was too late. She had lost a lot of blood. We the people know Daikini light and science, so I protected her body, in its physical shell, forever giving her my life force.

- You gave her your *Heka*... that's why you can't materialize... "

Taken by a wild hope, Andraste whispered.

"Lyra, if I gave her my life force...

- No. Magic can do a lot, but it can't bring the dead to life. Going against magic brings destruction."

Andraste gulped and touched the envelope made of tiny crystals all connected to each other, and noticed that her finger sank without breaking any. She stroked the medallion, trembling slightly and touching her mother's skin by grabbing the string that came undone without resistance. Andraste then withdrew her hand, gently, holding the jewel between her fingers. It was silly, but she had the feeling she disturbed the repose of the deceased. She noticed that the crystals were reformed and resumed their form instantly. Lyra spoke to her in a firmer voice.

"We need you to understand the outside world: they are afraid. And fear is the best way to take control over

72

someone. Never forget this, Andraste. You were born to fight, to defend this world, not to become a priestess and recite invocations. I promise you that in a few years when you are no longer the same, you might even be rejected because you will be so different from the others, you'll no longer see the world with the same eyes, and you'll no longer taste in the same way. You'll be different. You'll feel desperate sometimes, lost. You will be alone at the end, as we all are. But I promise you one thing: you will be strong. Nothing will bring you down, nothing and no one. You will conquer, by this force you have in you, you will conquer.

- What was her name?" Asked Andraste, still kneeling before the remains.

She twirled the medallion between her fingers, watching.

"I unfortunately don't know..."

Andraste then felt her throat tighten. The knowledge both so close, and lost forever plunged her into unspeakable sadness. It was so cold. So hard. Was it really her? Were these her features? What was her smile like? Andraste was lost in the contemplation of the face with relaxed features.

"Time passes, Andraste. Forty years have passed and Cassandra gave you two days.

- I'm listening." Sighed Andraste who felt her shoulders rise.

"The Sabians have created three medallions for three dominant races in this land. Here's one. We must discover its powers. This may be the most powerful relic that exists.

- How do we discover its powers?

- It came to you. It's chosen you. Only you can cast spells. Try levitation."

Focusing her mind on the medallion resting on her hand, the object remained flat.

"Reveal your powers by Iglal, the knowledge of god and of the night," she uttered, enclosing it between her palms.

Still nothing. Andraste then shrugged and tied it around her neck. Lyra looked at her in amazement.

"You ... your mind. It's as if it was closed. Like you've disappeared!

- Really?

- So it even protects your thoughts."

The novice swayed and put her hand to her forehead. Then, on her belly, just under her navel. She felt the presence of the Dagyde, far away in the Twin Mountains, Leprechauns sending all their hatred for humans, and a creature ... Andraste began to vomit.

"Lyra, I don't feel well. I ... I feel so much hate from all these magical creatures who have been tortured, persecuted...I feel it in me." She said, gasping.

The Daikini stood beside her. She stood just above the spiral of *Heka* of Dana's depths.

"Take it off. Here, it's too powerful, it could even become a weapon."

The novice obeyed, and stiffened. Blood ran between her thighs.

"You need to return to the foyer. You just started menstruating.

- Is it because of the medallion?

- Maybe so. I can teach you a lot of things, but you'll have to discover for yourself why the medallion happens to you... "

Andraste shuddered. She regretted the carelessness of some sixteen years ago. But the idea that she had a destiny was burning within her.

Chapter 7

Faraoh stood in front of the Senate court in his dark green coat, his regency pin attached to his shoulder. The Senators wore ostentatious purple robes, without an ounce of humility. Being a Senator was, after all, the highest office in the land of Hizaion.

"I now turn to you, noble Senators. And to you, Renova: I salute you."

He heard the crowd cheering outside. His lambs were massed in front of the giant screens that rebroadcast each session of the Senate. The people had the illusion of control in everything, including thinking they had access to all information.

"Do you remember the time the wolves wrought heinous carnage that devastated the provinces under the authority of the man in black?"

"Cursed is the name," he heard, in simmering agreement.

Tell them stories. Use images, evoke emotions. Faraoh was a master in the art of speech in the Assembly.

"Terrorizing the population, they used rape and abduction as pressure tactics when villagers didn't want to cooperate and give up everything they had. The Sokar rebels, half human, half-reptile creatures, shared the same strategy of terror as the other magical creatures, not by conviction, but by using the taste of fear and blood! Looting goods and crops. They eroded the land, rounding up humans as booty between each attack: between two and six women, with or without children. Do you remember, my brothers? Some were sold as slaves, others, the weak, having been tortured, were terminated. As for the captives, they had to prepare food, fetch water, and carry the loot of the warriors. They even carried their children, poor cadavers they couldn't bear to abandon. Entire villages were emptied. It was a horrible exodus for the villagers, and for those poor girls who sometimes succeeded in escaping. Wandering at random, they sought out the fate of any town they could: Would it be safe and sound? Or already devastated? Hungry and weak, they sometimes carried, in addition to their misery, one or two of their children, abducted at the same time as them, survivors of an atrocious rape. They were bastards, sometimes half human. It was then that they were rejected by the communities who considered them soiled."

The images were like powerful seeds planted in the collective unconscious of his audience. They created ripples on the surface of the water, and finally, waves.

"A wave of assassins! Then, with the king's blessing, rest his soul, I formed the Militia: mercenaries yes, but the revolt drove away the looters and gangs. They also foiled the plots of those who had blown on the embers of hatred that the creatures of the ancient world bore against humans: the priests and their apprentices. We wanted to deal with the leaders of the coup, but they would hear nothing: all these degenerate monsters who wanted to exterminate us ... They wanted to storm the city of Samatya. Supported by the elves, the former "allies and protectors" of humans. Then it happened— the great battle."

The words slipped out of Faraoh's mouth. The words were the sceptre, which Faraoh had wielded since the beginning of his conquest for power. They were fascinated by his words. He was redrawing history and changing the people's perception. A word. How could such a fickle and inconsistent thing as the wind, create gusts of hatred and submission? That, according to Faraoh, was magic.

"Certainly, I am not perfect. I failed to fully satisfy you, oh people. I hadn't planned for the cunning priests and their evil shield. I hadn't expected the cowardly murder of the Royal Family by dissidents... If only my wife... "

Faraoh bowed his head, his features in a grimace.

"My wife, your princess Phanéa, who we all loved, gave birth to an heir before dying in childbirth twenty five years ago..."

A stunned silence followed. Yes, all the royalty was dead, but one didn't just dismiss traditions with the wave of a hand. He'd obeyed the people, taking the King's daughter for his companion and founding a dynasty, ensuring the continuity of power and thus the security in the country. The people missed the unity the royalty had instilled for centuries, for everyone, for people that were so different from one another. But today, only humans remained.

"My regency must end."

A flurry of emotion stirred in the Senate. The crowd outside roared.

"I modernized the city in only a few decades. I partly built the city of Renova over the old city, whose name we no longer pronounce, and I civilized the New World. I put my knowledge, my science, to the service of Renova to ensure your food, your water, your safety, your harmonious development through new births, through security, and the designation of city members. The regency must end. My dynasty shall not be a part of the crimes committed by our royalty.

Everyone held their breath. But a member of the congregation cried, without rising:

"And the forest? The priests? They'll form a resistance with their magic! If you go, what will become of us?

- The priority is to maintain order in the lower city, as the forest is probably empty. Our eyes need to focus beyond the walls of the city, and regain the lost territories between Rosendal and Renova."

Removing his son, the heir, from Renova had been the trickiest part to carry out. Citing the threat of dissidents, he had sent him off to be educated from-soldiers serving in the rear guard of the Militia. Kings were usually educated by priests and elves: there, in the island military fortress of the north, his son had learned weaponry. Today, he was back to help him establish his authority once and for all on the Senate.

"Neither King, nor regent. We need a new order for a new and strong world. New bases, new institutions, new laws. It will become a great country, and a powerful republic that I promise to carry far and high. This is my gift! Renova, I ask you today: do you still want me to be your servant?" Asked Faraoh, eyes closed, palms open to the sky as a sign of offering.

It wasn't a speech, it was a prayer. A prayer to the gods. One must always let the crowd speak for itself, and not the individuals giving the speech. This gives them the impression of being gods, when they're in reality, sacrificial lambs. The crowd roared outside. Elijah had recently obtained the post of Senator of the Northern provinces, and had whispered the perfect name of suggestion to the influential members. The Senators raised their hands to elect Faraoh as Guardian of the Nation.

The elf clenched his fists to jumpstart his circulation. Days, weeks, months, years. Locked up here.

Tortured. Mutilated. Then his limb would grow back: sometimes, it took days, sometimes weeks. Everything depended on what they forced him to ingest. He was the perfect guinea pig for Faraoh's experiments.

"I would have preferred a female ... To measure the differences with human gestation. I had to content myself with Phanéa for my experiments, which failed miserably elsewhere. No one is perfect."

Lyander, eyes striated with blood by fatigue, watched Faraoh, reading a document on a sheet. He pouted.

"My dear, we're going to have to part."

The last son of Goiri watched him while he drummed his fingers on a machine that was as pristine as the jail.

"The time has passed so quickly," sighed the master of the city, pulling on the tail of his white coat.

He swirled the light solution and emptied it in one gulp.

"Well, I know that for you elves, time is nothing. That's why I've pampered you. I waited patiently for you to come back. You can't imagine how much I was looking forward to seeing and working with you. But for a prince of your rank, you do come from a royal line after all, I wanted ... to find you a room that was worthy. Yes... "

He looked around thoughtfully with admiration.

"I managed to transform this city. ... And I'll transform the entire country."

He got up and came towards Lyander, separating each strand of his hair. He bent over the elf who struggled to articulate.

"Traitor ... You will pay."

Faraoh burst into a loud laugh.

"Really? It's as if you're telling me a story from one of your ragged bards!"

Faraoh felt the weight of the elf's wrists in his hands, surprised.

"Yes I've come to the end of my little experiments on you. Administration of the blood of different creatures, electric treatment, electromagnetic shock... "

In doing so, Faraoh pressed down on a button that swung the chair, causing Lyander to face the door.

"I thank you from the bottom of my heart. I have a few last questions for you before giving you a mission. Are the elves are telepathic?

- Why?

- Can you get in touch with the Sabians? Did you manage to contact them when you were in Rosendal?

- Suck it!

Faraoh clenched his teeth.

"What rudeness. I expected more elegance from an elf. They say it was you who started spreading poetry in these lands. Moving on. I know that the Sabians possess immortality. You elves live for hundreds of years, but the Sabians ... Tell me. What is their secret?

- I promise you I'll be the one who will roll your head to Iglal's feet.

- The gods have deserted the country. I am the new god, Faraoh said softly.

Lyander noticed how the years had had no effect on the master of the city.

"Well, one last sample, I wouldn't want to have any regrets when I let you go!"

Lyander winced as the knife that sank into his flesh.

"I'll leave you alone a few days, just to give you some time, and after that, you'll go and fulfil my mission."

He gently wiped a cloth on his forehead, beaded with sweat.

"You'll go to Etheldrede for me. I've searched all over the lands of Hizaion discreetly to avoid arousing suspicion. But now I need it. You call it a relic ... So here's a hint: I've never seen it, but it's probably the most powerful relic of all...

- Why would I help you? What makes you think I'll return and that I won't just stay there?

- You have nothing left: only that desire for revenge that keeps you alive. And, if you don't do it, I'll kill everyone here. Soon I won't need them. I'm trying to create my perfect citizens. Obedient to the eye ... and to the finger."

Faraoh smiled, waving his index finger.

"Imagine thousands of lives in this city destroyed, and it all being your fault. The battle that your father miserably lost would be only a taste of what you'd reap.

He pressed the button that opened the door, and Faraoh went out with a satisfied smile. Lyander, exhausted, felt himself relax, and fell asleep.

"The four pillars of magic are?

- To know, to will, to dare... "

The young novice held her head in her hands, perched in the tree next to Cassandra.

"Keep quiet! This is the easiest! And the four pillars of the temple are?

- Silence, intelligence, depth, and truth."

This part was easier because Andraste associated the words by visualizing the primitive temple and the statues inside.

"What will happen on the day of initiation if you are not able to answer the questions of the Elders?

- I hope I'll be judged on anything other than the recitation."

The magician remained speechless.

"I find you're becoming very insolent, Andraste."

The girl bit her lip. But she found that Cassandra had also changed her attitude since her return. Was it because of her bleeding? Or ... Andraste wore the medallion around her neck more and more, hiding it under her clothes. Cassandra had tried several times to enter her mind like she never had before. But she'd hit a wall. Even now, she felt like she was outside of herself, trying to listen to the murmur of her thoughts, in vain. Andraste felt increasingly uncomfortable with the vow of obedience and belonging to the caste. She was a person, dammit! She was entitled to some privacy!

"Do you know why there is an initiation ceremony? Why is it so sacred?"

- It's like a birthday, I suppose."

Cassandra watched the girl. Since that day, she was no longer the same. Was it the encounter with the tree, or the arrival of her period? She had been called by the Yew, one of the sacred trees of the forest land of Hizaion ... She closed her mind quickly and became totally sealed. She seemed more detached, her vague gaze lost in the Azur. She'd tried at night when her mind was more receptive, but Andraste disappeared as well ... None of this reassured the priestess, who was following the advice of Aygulf to carefully distil the knowledge of priests. Who was she really? Was it a simple teenage authority crisis? Or even a reincarnated being charged with a high task? It was also the same question that the young novice was asking herself at this precise moment.

"No. An initiation is a death. And a rebirth into the Caste. You'll really understand who you are at this moment. The initiate receives the force of the stars and the earth simultaneously.

- Meaning?" asked Andraste. She felt the hesitation of the sorceress.

"The initiation happens in a place where the *Heka* is concentrated and powerful. This is a huge burden the insider receives. Those who hadn't worked on their inner discipline and mental strength couldn't resist, and went crazy."

The novice shuddered. The priestess clapped her hands.

"Come on! Let's practice!"

At the edge of the river, Cassandra leaned on a stick and pounded the ground, a few meters behind her protégée.

"Again!"

86

Andraste inhaled deeply:

"Heka tah berendil mirthyo ...

- Mirthyo pusha!

- Oh yes, *Heka tah berendil mirthyo pusha!"*

Andraste felt the impatience of her guardian. She was sorry to disappoint her, she for whom everything had always been easy. But remembering all these formulas, feeling the *Heka* project from her mind, pouring all her strength into her wand—it was too difficult. She felt her throat tighten. She'd never get there. Lyra was wrong. She was nothing special. She was an orphan taken out of charity by priests. Cassandra was distraught by such disobedience. She found herself wanting to grab her hair and slap her. So much talent wasted by a lack of obedience and ill will! She couldn't just end her novitiate, what could she do? Send her to Rosendal?

Lyra appeared in the mind of the girl. Cassandra saw with amazement Andraste let down her wand and raised her hands as if to form a shield. Then the water rose, slowly dripping on the pebbles who lie naked in the river bed. The young novice, head bent forward, used her hands to levitate the water ... and suddenly, in a flash, she projected it forward in a concentrated stream. When she turned, Cassandra contemplated her with dilated eyes, subdued ... or frightened.

Chapter 8

The two militia soldiers jeered.

"Grilled elf, we've never eaten this at Renova!"

While the first detached him from his chains, the second looked at his milky shield with admiration. He put out his hand fearfully, and grazed it with his fingertips. He received a shock that caused his heart to jump. His finger was burnt. He stepped back, shaking his head.

"Luckily we caught you in the old city. What were you doing there, huh? You have a mission? You've already forgotten the ole pig's head?"

He said, slapping his neck. The second was still looking at his finger and whispering to himself:

"This place is cursed." He turned towards his colleague, holding Lyander by the hair, and blocking his arm behind his back, slipping his head into the Azur. The elf let out a terrible scream. It was worse than all his torture. The two militiamen pushed him out completely, and Lyander entered Etheldrede.

Days. Weeks. Months? How long had he been there? Was he walking on the sun? The images rattled in his head. The light was too bright. The ground under his feet too far. He couldn't feel his arms. He felt disjointed. His throat was too tight. He was breathing heavily, bending to the ground.

The face of his father appeared. The noble Goiri ordering him to rally reinforcements from the south and west. He wore the proud badge of the Royal Guard. He would find the Sabians. At the head of a formidable army of tens of thousands of men, he'd defeat Faraoh and his pitiful army of mercenaries. The proud face of his father. It wasn't real. It was an image that was passing among others. Lyander stopped, bowing more. The light was gone. The soft green foliage was less aggressive. A Dagyde suddenly sprang up, screaming and attacked Lyander. Unable to fight, staggering under the blows, trying to protect his head, he collapsed. The Dagyde sniffed a few moments, pounded his body half unconscious and then fled. Lyander called out to the old gods, who didn't have names, in a silent prayer. This was the only moment of clarity in Lyander's mind before submerging in an endless night. The forest alone would not suffice to heal the body and mind of the broken elf.

The novice was walking along a river, her waist belted with a coarse rope. She was dragging a large stone, barefoot. Cassandra was punishing her for daring to touch the books of the upper floor of the library. But this dream she kept having... Andraste wanted to understand it: a Dagyde that melted, an elf feeding on a white doe ... she'd say nothing to Cassandra. If she had willingly shared her dreams with her guardian before, nothing would have been like it is today. She felt a furious need to understand it by itself.

"I can't stand it, Lyra!"

She sat on a flat stone that bordered the river, catching her breath.

"Repeat what I've taught you...

- The key to magic is the formula. Sounds that have been repeated for millennia are full of *Heka.* Certain powerful words are even equivalent to a whole spell.

- Get up."

Andraste stood, grinning. The cord warmed her skin through a rabbit-skin tunic. Cassandra had even deprived her of food this morning. But the punishments only kindled her desire to learn ... and to surpass her guardian.

"Do you remember the one that I showed you the first time?"

Andraste saw the image of the dead leaf brought back to life, which passed through the elements without burning up.

"Look at the bottom of the river. What do you see?"

- There's no more algae.

- We'll fix it. Repeat after me. *Abraxas.*

-. *Abraxas* Will it bring them back to life?

- Yes. It's used to infuse *Heka*. It revives what's inanimate. Or freezes it for eternity."

The girl watched nearby:

"Cassandra is busy milking the goat. She's not watching you.

- I feel more and more suspicious of her trying to control me.

- I know. You have to understand Andraste, she serves the Caste. She only obeys the Council. She's doing her best.

- She's been anxious for several days.

- What do you mean?

- It's like she's on guard. As if she's watching for danger.

- Yes, the forest changes to protect herself too. I've noticed it too. The trees move like their covering their tracks, didn't you notice?

- Yes." admitted the girl...

She watched the water of the river for a moment. Then she got up and placed her hands before her, pronouncing the formula. Nothing happened. Andraste untied the rope from her waist. It was too hot to walk and carry the weight at the same time.

"How do I do this?" She asked, annoyed.

- Use the formula. Concentrate on the place right below the navel.

Andraste breathed deeply to calm herself. Lyra's teachings were too precious. The novice tried again. She imagined one algae, then several, soon lining the bottom of the river. She felt her *Heka* drop. She weakened. She suddenly felt angry. Anger against the Caste who slowed her progress. Anger against her parents for having left her alone in this world. Anger against Lyra for sometimes leaving her alone. Anger against herself for not being able to do it right the first time. She felt grief. Despair. What's the point? She didn't even know where to go... Her chest was so heavy. She had one goal: to integrate into the Caste. But what about after? Where would she go? She'd be torn from the forest she'd always known. Charged with a mission she no longer believed in ...And all of this was Faraoh's fault. He should be killed. If only someone could kill him ... her eyes still closed, her rage returned:

"Andraste! No!!"

The novice lost the thread of her spell which was interrupted. She lowered her hands. Her head was heavy and dizzy. She'd done it! A brown seaweed carpeted the bottom of the river.

"It should have been green...

- What ... what has happened? Did I succeed?

- Yes and no. You're not able to control yourself. Anger, grief. All living beings have felt them."

Andraste looked piteously his feet. She'd never get there.

"You'll get there. You have to. You have to keep the balance. That's what the forest does. That's what magic does: it keeps a balance in the world, which always threatens to descend into

chaos.

- And I was the chaos.

- You breathed in the *Heka* of the algae and the water itself... "

The young novice felt bad watching the river. It seemed to her that the water level had dropped.

"The medallion of Anjara protects your mind, but only you can protect your heart."

The girl was suddenly tired. Her flower had probably come back.

"I need to be alone, Lyra" she told the Daikini.

And the light at her side disappeared without a word.

She stood in front of the temple of Hizaion, thoughtfully. She opened the door and slid in slowly. She wanted to see her mother, lie down beside her, and contemplate her eternal sleep. She wanted to watch the temple ceiling and secret messages that glowed in the dark. She wanted to persuade herself that what was written was her destiny, and that she would only need a little time before she could read and achieve it. But as soon as she was inside, she felt something different. The door had closed behind her!

"We're not alone," Whispered Lyra, who had returned.

"Come!" And she opened her secret passage.

Andraste went down and ran through the halls, tense, her hair spiking up on her body. She was scared. Lyra tried to reassure her:

"They change every opening so that the malicious person remains trapped and lost forever."

If attacked, Lyra could protect her. Andraste progressed slowly but surely, under the guidance of Lyra. Suddenly, she was in the hall of mirrors. How was that possible? She hadn't even climbed the stairs! Plunging into darkness, she pinned herself against a wall. Something moved in the darkness. A hideous creature like from her nightmares, gray with pockmarked skin drawn over bones that protruded from its body. Its huge wings folded and formed a strange angle. It was bald, with non-existent ears ... But the most disgusting thing, was its grunt. It was bent over the shroud of her mother, which it devoured. Andraste took a breath, still in darkness, and slid to the side. She walked along the wall. The passage had closed behind her ... She had to find another way, or attack the thing from behind. It was her only chance. Holding her breath, she slipped her shoes on the wet ground soundlessly.

"It's going to smell me..." she said mentally to Lyra.

Suddenly, her foot lightly brushed against a slab. The creature looked up and unfurled its wings, bloodshot eyes fixing on

Andraste. She moved forward coldly, leading with her novice dagger. She had no fear. She was angry, she was furious. She was ready to fight and shed the blood of the monster that disturbed the repose of her mother. No, she wouldn't die tonight. She wouldn't back down. She was cruelly gleaming her blade in the dim light. She wasn't a child, she held her dagger, glittering and vengeful. The creature pulled back, fixing its red and white eyes on the girl, walking away from her mother's body, stepping aside. She saw the clawed arms and scrawny legs, its ribs torn in injury. Suddenly, the creature flew away. It was a Tengu. The creature had disappeared into the darkness of the vault. Andraste thought: they preferred to go out at night, as they didn't perceive the same sounds as humans, they were great warriors but fought as mercenaries who paid well ... Andraste stared at the darkness. How far down did the sanctuary underground go? Suddenly, she was attacked by the Tengu. It fell upon her, and the novice barely had time to dodge. She screamed: the creature had scratched her back. She had to get up ... she had to. She tried to parry her way out, but the blow was coming. The creature, moving faster, hit her in the face. The girl felt the dagger fly out of his hands. The Tengu planted it in her in a split second, letting out a screech. Andraste doubled over, her ears torn and painful. Then the creature leaned towards her. It was good two meters high.

"Sweet virgin ... I'll have your blood and your medallion. It's all I need to reach my people and find my place."

She had to procrastinate, to save time. Lyra, dematerialized, couldn't help her. She spotted her dagger on the floor in front of the right wall. She straightened completely and put all her weight back on her right leg.

"What's your name?

- Hiero. I am the leader of the Tengu. Who will I have the honor of killing and eating tonight?"

But Andraste had shifted her weight to her standing leg and drove a tremendous kick to its stomach. It was just enough to make it step a few steps back. She rolled over and grabbed the dagger. When she turned, he was on it. She plunged her dagger into its belly. Hiero stopped short. It screamed, trying to breathe, but it was suffocating. In his agony, it stared intently at the medallion with his red eyes. Andraste pushed him away and ran breathlessly. Lyra was there before her eyes, fragile but a persistent light in the darkness, guiding her toward the exit.

Andraste felt the breath of the wings of Hiero behind her. She dived out of the temple and closed the door yelling the closing spell:

"Méhata!!"

He was trapped. Her lungs were going to explode, her legs would give way. The wound in her back was horribly painful. The Tengu healed quickly, as one couldn't kill them with a simple dagger... They'd see each other again, that was certain. She stepped back, thinking about how fortunate she was to have survived.

She prepared a mixture of mint and rosemary she always kept in her room with honey. Cassandra most likely wouldn't assign her a chore tomorrow. Andraste heard a twig snap behind her. She thought her heart was going to stop, turning to discover an individual with his bow strung.

An elf stood before her, jaws clenched, ready to attack, cheeks clenched. He face was long and scarred, and he had long blond hair tied into a ponytail. A being from another world, beyond the Azur, from the land of Hizaion that had been forgotten by her and the healer ... She asked:

"Who are you?"

He blinked as if it were an interior struggle and stood hunched over, like an animal. He pulled his bow, but she had time to hide behind a stone. She hesitated and grabbed a stone that was lying on the floor. Andraste unsheathed her sling and shot him in the face. The stone hit him in the forehead, causing him to cry in pain. The girl in was on him in seconds, pushing him with kicks, unsheathing the sword of the elf to keep him distracted as she regained her senses.

"Who are you? What do you want?!"

Lyander didn't hear her: his night vision was interrupted by the blow to his head ... *She was standing there within reach of my sword, where did she go? Kill. He had to kill her.*

He pulled another arrow, roaring. Andraste suddenly flicked her wrist, and averted the arrow.

The elf continued to advance, determined, and silence fell in the clearing. He drew a second arrow, which Andraste again deflected. He drew a third, a fourth, a fifth, but Andraste deflected all of them with the sword. They faced each other, tensely. He reached for another arrow, but had no more.

"The sun's setting, sir. I suggest you state the purpose of your visit if you want to spend the night protected."

The elf looks at the clouds. The sun, before dying in the horizon stroked its most beautiful colors on the elf's scarred face. He was a wild beauty, breath-taking. Aside from her crazy eyes ... Why did he attack her? The elf dropped his bow, growling.

"What? What'd you say?"

He took out his dagger and crouched like a cat assessing the weak point of its prey. Then he fixed his eyes on his sword. He was stronger than she was, and she hadn't been trained in combat. But what if she cast a spell?

"Lyra! What should I do?"

She saw the light on her right radiate slowly. The elf tried to resist the light. Then he looked like he was hypnotized. Lyra was talking to him! Andraste couldn't distinguish their murmurs, but the elf put away his dagger.

"Lyra, what did you say to him?

- I took care of him. Go away Andraste! Go home!"

The elf hesitated, looking again Andraste, who stepped to the side. But Lyra was stronger, and peeling his attention away, he fled westward toward the twin mountains Indra and Bashat. Was he really the elf she'd dreamed of? Why'd drink the milk of a doe? He seemed able to hunt ... Why had he attacked her?

That evening, after having concealed Lyander's sword under her bed, she dreamed of the full moon, and an elf with blue eyes that pierced her skin.

Chapter 9

The healer felt weakened after her trip. She didn't sleep well for a few days, haunted by her impending interview. The room was poorly decorated, considering the circumstances. A statuette of Dana, the Mother, made of red clay and crowned with flowers sat in front of the priests and sages in the center. The rest of the gods encircled, also represented by various figures. They were roughly carved out of wood and painted in different colors. Where were the other sages? There were only two: Aman, eternally dressed in his white tunic and rarely cheerful blue eyes, ever mindful, sunk in their sockets. His hands on his belly, his expressionless eyes were fixed on her. He was sitting in one of the five seats in the room. To his right stood Wyre, tall and straight, also dressed in white. She had cut her jet black hair, which suited her beautifully and showed off her ebony eyes. Cassandra presented Andraste's horoscope. She then spoke of the undeniable qualities of the novice suited to the religious path. Aygulf and Ferens a few steps down, stood before the two sages, their leaders, and listened attentively. Then came the presentation of the design. It was a test that all the children wishing to join the Caste of priests had to pass, but who hadn't been chosen at the time of the Seeding, the annual selection. A silence followed the presentation of the painting. Aman arose, and observed the painting more closely. The instructions were the same for all: one needed three circles of different sizes, progressing from smallest to largest.

Only Sages could read the sacred drawings: it was like reading someone's mind.

"I guess she didn't have much choice in colors...

- No, it's true that the red is dominant, but...

- Yes yes, we know, we'll consider this in our decision."

Andraste had used a lot of red, green, and purple. The purple was dark enough to give a slightly disturbing look to the piece, with the contrast of the white background washed over the parchment. But Aman looked at something else in detail, stroking the bridge of his nose and chin: Andraste had outlined her dotted drawing. They were red dots, thin but numerous, forming a spiral around the circle drawing.

"How was parchment positioned, Cassandra?

- Like this, oh Aman."

As she presented the parchment to the Sage the spiral ascended. Better to remain silent than to snort at the novice's results. The dots were the only part where Andraste had put a certain application, in order to completely cover the pattern of three circles. But on closer look, it was true that the circles disappeared under the orderly myriad of particles invading the empty space. Cassandra found the design hypnotic. She had never seen anything like it. Aman opened his mouth then, then changed his mind. Wyre continued:

"And you say you do not know who her parents are?

- Yes.

- How can we be sure they won't reclaim her?

- I think they're dead, oh Sage. I believe they hid the child in the forest before heading south along the river."

Aman sat back down, keeping the parchment in his hand. Aygulf even dared to slip him his usual confident smile. Aman decided to speak, rubbing the parchment between his thumb and forefinger:

"An outstanding personality ... from what I can see …just as I've been told."

Aygulf must have warned them about Andraste's difficulties with authority.

"This child is surrounded by obscurity. The conditions related to her birth. Her abandonment in the forest ... I focused on her intensely, but I don't see anything. I don't see her mind.

- She recently acquired the ability to protect her thoughts.

- Is it you who taught her?

- No ... oh Sage Aman.

- You should test her, Cassandra. What I mean is, you have to put her in perilous situations, and her spirit will be reflected in her actions. We'll see if she can really claim to be on our side."

Andraste slipped through the window at night, making sure not to make any noise, walking barefoot on the thatched roof. She ran, ran towards Lyra, who was waiting at the ancient temple. She inhaled the perfumes that the forest exhaled. She wasn't afraid, she was vibrating with excitement. What would the Daikini teach her today? A few days ago, Cassandra had made her read books on regenerative potions. She felt that Cassandra was trying to revive her spiralling interest. Lyra had allowed Andraste to reverse roles: it wasn't she who was in demand to know, but the Council who needed recruits ... however they were, whatever their age.

Of course, arriving near the temple, she saw no one. Lyra only showed herself with the light of the moon Sothya. The clouds passed, and the blue orb appeared in all its magnificence, close and majestic. Lyra appeared on a rock under the cover of night. Andraste had come to recognize her better and better, perceiving that she had a body that reflected colors of lemon yellow, gold, and purple.

"Andraste, you're going to meet your protector animal. This is normally assigned to a certain class of priests, but you need to have the odds on your side.

- What will it do for me?

- It will protect you. When I'm gone."

Andraste realized that Lyra had sacrificed a great deal for her.

She'd never see her family…

"Very good. Now sing the name of the god Aum, father of all things."

Andraste chanted a few minutes, feeling her body become increasingly heavy. She saw a white light, pure and silvery, emerge from the ground, which then entered into her by her feet. She felt light move up along her spine up to her head, then falling like rain around her body. The process continued over and over. The young apprentice saw an envelope form around her, shimmering. It wasn't rain, it was a waterfall, a shield that had formed around her. Lyra let her enjoy the sensation for a while, the feeling of pure protection unleashed by the *Heka*.

"Now, turn to your left and walk as much as you want. You'll come to a clearing where you'll find an apple tree. I'll meet you there."

Andraste did as Lyra told her. There, she realized she knew little about this part of the forest, and she promised herself to explore it more in the future. In the shadows at the foot of the apple tree, she suddenly detected movement. A dark character, strong, dressed in a dark green tunic that blended with the wooden crown on his head, stood with a club in his hands. Andraste didn't feel reassured.

"It's the wild herder, the keeper of the animals. He'll summon your protector animal."

Andraste greeted the man with the deference Cassandra had spoken of. No one knew if he was a human or a god. He didn't speak, appearing and disappearing at will. He looked at her with a neutral eye, but Andraste felt no particular sympathy from him. What a strange being... then the wild herder struck his stick against the tree. Suddenly, she heard a cry. A falcon. It appeared in the air, circling above her as if to make her admire its pure beauty. It was a *Horehim*, a falcon of the south, with green and black feathers. A loner.

He settled on a low branch of a spruce. The stars had disappeared. Only the Sothya moon shone, wrapping the bird in a ceremonial dress. The two creatures watched. Andraste whistled. The hawk ignored her, preferring to scrape the tree branch. It was useless to call it, even if she whistled while raising her arms, her falcon didn't care. The wild herder had disappeared, and Lyra was invisible. Andraste took a deep breath, then walked right up to him.

Fifty meters separated her from the volatile beast. The falcon then fixed his piercing eyes on her and spread its wings. He took off and soared. Andraste stopped running and stood in the middle of the plain, with gaping eyes on the dark night. Suddenly, he nosed-dived, and rushed towards Andraste. The girl smiled and raised her arm. But the bird didn't spread his wings to stop and rest on the perch offered. He accelerated his crashing descent.

"I should have taken my athame for defense ... He's going to poke my eyes out," thought Andraste. Perhaps he was testing to see if she would be worthy of him.

But the *Horehim* barely curved its trajectory and fell upon her. It was a shock: she felt the bird pass though her like a current, like a wave unfurling water droplets in the river. Time slowed and decomposed. An immense heat in her chest spread through her, as she no longer controlled her movements. She'd become the falcon. She saw herself hovering above the clouds, embracing the earth and its horizon, lord of the sky. She felt the wind gliding under her feathers, taken by the lightness and euphoria of being carried away by the wind, watching miles of land, fields, and rivers. She felt the different currents of the world circulate in the air. She'd felt it under her feet, and they were there, in the secret passages of *Heka*. Then, she felt herself falling. She spun and fell back into her body. Had she only left for a moment?

Andraste remained on her back, watching the falcon twirl and disappear behind the trees. She knew that the animal didn't belong to her. Another link, even more powerful, was created that night. *Morphnée*. It had a nice ring. He'd told her his name.

Lyra reappeared at her side. Lying in the grass beside her, speaking through the dew, she left to Andraste time to regain her senses.

"He'll come back whenever you're in need. Boldness and truth are his qualities."

Andraste felt the world spin, feeling the movement of stars leaving their majestic contrails in the sky. Her heartbeat slowed until it became nearly imperceptible. She saw the infinite cosmos, the celestial tree that held all the worlds, draining *Heka* from its new seeds.

"We don't change forms, but we do identify with the creature, as you did with your falcon. They give us a deeper awareness, sharpen our world around us and intervene when we ask them. You can do the same thing with the elements: water, earth, fire, air ... We're in constant contact with the invisible world, and we remain a part of it. Nature is never hostile because we are its guardians. But sometimes it incurs an action to restore balance to its plans, its forces and its energy. This is the same *Heka* that drives us, that vibrates beneath the surface within us. The sap that rises in the trees, the water that rushes and always finds its way, the human who unfolds himself to the world, the light that makes me shimmer and then appear ... This is *Heka* circulating around us, creating a gigantic web of life. We're all one by it. Do you understand that, Andraste?

- I think so...

- Get up. Let's try something else."

Lyra asked her to close her eyes and spin around three times. She had to start looking for a lake.

"There's a lake? Cassandra never told me about a lake!

- You'll see for yourself!"

The girl felt like she was swaying. She wandered a while, then stopped. She inhaled deeply several times, and suddenly, turned to the left and plunged into the forest to the south east. She walked, then began to run, run. Suddenly she bumped against a tree, then another! Her head was spinning, and she'd bruised her hands and twisted her ankle in the crevice between the stones. Lyra was at her side. She zigzagged through the trees, trying to stay the course.

"Faster, faster Andraste!"

She accelerated. She no longer felt her pulse, her dry throat, her painful joints. Her feet traced the paths intuitively, avoiding rocks, crevices, brambles, and roots coming out of the ground, like slippery foam. She didn't need to see or feel, he body was one with the surrounding nature.

Lyra spoke to her in her head now. Could it be?

"Life isn't a straight line. It is a spiral, that of the life cycle. It's about accomplishing, gravitating. The path of magic is to explore with your mind these trails. We are the heart of the forest, and the entire universe, and every time we aim to discover something, we do it, we accomplish it. It's not a question of acquiring knowledge, but daring to go into the deeper levels of the mind."

Andraste no longer existed, rather, she was one with an immense force that propelled her. She sped through the trees at an exhilarating speed. She felt her body exude a tremendous heat. Inner fire rose, and exhaled through her skin and clothing. The lake was near. She'd soon feel the pebbles. She accelerated again. But suddenly, the ground beneath her feet disappeared. Between heaven and earth, Andraste experience a moment of sheer delight. She felt the sensation of the falcon spreading its wings once more. But she began to fall and was afraid: what if she fell into the crystal quarry? Andraste felt her pulse accelerate abruptly, and blood pounded in her temples and in her arms. She had no idea what position she'd land in. To die like this, would be too silly. The impact took her breath away.

Lyander looked up and let go of the udder. The white doe rose elegantly and darted her soft black eyes. The elf wiped the milk flowing from his mouth, and blinked when his pupils were dilated. Suddenly the girl appeared, blindfolded, running at full speed through the trees. Lyander snorted and went steeply in pursuit. When he saw her jump, he paused a moment and looked stunned for a few minutes, squatting on the stone which surmounted the lake ... The girl wasn't coming back up.

The water was icy. Thermal shock had to have killed her. Words and ideas rattled in his head. He was worried, and squealed like a wolf, probing the depths of the water. Unable to wait, he dove. He spotted her, a fragile flower resting gently among the stones, hair draped like a corolla. He swam to her quickly, and hoisted her to the surface to bring her ashore.

She was unconscious and not breathing. He began to cry out, pressing on her chest. He needed to see it rise and fall. She had to breathe. He pushed on her chest, then began to strike it. Still nothing. Suddenly, an idea flashed through his mind. He took his knife and cut his forearm, wincing in pain.

Lyander set the girl's face in his lap and applied his pen to the wound at her mouth. He imbibed her lips, and with his finger, placed the liquid on her tongue. Andraste's emerald eyes snapped open, turning blue, circled in black. The elf stared in her eyes as she clung to his arm greedily, sucking the blood from his wound. She closed her eyes. It was a taste that was both familiar and indefinable. Someone had pulled her out of darkness, forcing her to open her eyes to a blinding light. Her veins radiated, burning from the inside. Pain, delight. Someone held her. She released her grip and gave way to the heat of the body, feeling safe. The superhuman forces that had brought her back began to dull. Lyander lifted her and carried the girl to his shelter. Lyra had guided him to the old village of Loires and Braque: a village made of huts in the trees and connected by rope bridges. He lay her down on his bed of leaves where she dreamed of her falcon and drinking a chalice filled with a silver-colored liquid...

She awoke with a start within hours. The elf was sitting on the floor, leaning against the wall. He tried to calm her. The images stopped scrolling in her head. She tried to put the pieces of the puzzle in place.

"You ... you saved me?"

He didn't answer, dragging his fingers along the grooves of a wooden board.

"Thank you. Do… do you hear me? "

It was like talking to a wild animal. Like a wolf who growled and whose language she didn't' understand. She rose slowly. The door was ajar and it was still dark.

His headache returned, grabbing his hair and forcing his head back. The voice. Focus on the voice.

"What are you doing here? What happened to you?"

Questions. Always questions. Then come the burning. Then came the mutilation. And then come the blood: the chimera of blood, the blood of Tengus, the blood of Tomtes, fairy blood ... it would make him drink all kinds of blood. And they watched. And asked him questions. Always questions.

"What happened to you?" Andraste asked softly.

The elf braced himself against the wall with a roar, making them, clawing at the air, as if he plagued by an invisible opponent trying to attack him. Andraste sprang forward and ran away.

Chapter 10

"I'm going to teach you something today, Andraste."

The young girl gritted her teeth, following her tutor. It was the word "today" that annoyed her. Lyra, who believed in her, methodically taught her magic day after day. Without the Council, without the Order, she'd begun on the Sacred Path, following her initiation. They walked in silence for a few minutes, until they arrived at a crossroads. It emitted a special light. Andraste wanted to ask her about the lesson of the day, but Cassandra took her arm, rendering her silent. The day pierced the top of the foliage: from under the roots, emerged butterflies with fiery wings and quivering colors. Deities of the wind, stars of morning and the timid twilight, the butterflies awakened to visit the earth incognito. Soft and radiant, they were flying in the air, clinging, seeking, loitering and caressing the air, timid and draped in colors like beautiful plumed banners. Their show was amazing. Andraste began to breathe in unison with the butterflies. Cassandra sat on a stone at the foot of the tree.

"The butterfly lives between light and shadow. It's the ultimate symbol of reincarnation, from cocoon to caterpillar. It represents those who search for the light, who leave this barren and sterile world. We need to move towards the heavenly and flourishing world. It represents love because it asks for nothing in return: condemned to a short life, it's at the opposite spectrum of the gods. The butterfly is a servant of the light which it reflects and sends out to the world. Yet, he's the companion of death, prowling the darkness. Reincarnated as butterflies, these beings carry messages from the beyond, from the invisible world, to us. The noblest task is to respond to them and to do the will of the gods, so they'll reward us."

Andraste said nothing, watching the motley insects and the curls they made in the air.

"I know that you'd like to start your initiation right away, Andraste. But my hands are tied because of the Council...

- I understand," said Andraste, between her teeth.

What bothered her, was that, although Lyra had initiated her, she still needed help to find her kind. And outside the forest of Etheldrede, the world was vast: she didn't know which way to go or what powers she'd have. She had to admit, she needed the Caste.

"I can feel you distancing yourself, Andraste, and our friendship ... I know you're sad; you prefer to be alone in the forest. But I can still give you some hints. Today, I'll teach you divination by butterflies.

- I apologize for my disobedience, Cassandra. This last step prior to the initiation is not easy for me, I must confess."

The girl sat next to Cassandra. Insects were flying around them, foraging flowers without paying attention to their presence.

"See the *Tiger Swallowtail* with his orange and sometimes gray dress? He brings harmony between your desires and what will come. He's the proclamation of love. This other one, the mottled yellow and black one, means the opposite: malaise, an ambiguous situation, a disappointment. This is a *Lys of Decorum.* That one that landed on the branch there is a *Gem of Mimosa.* When he comes flying close to you, it indicates success if you follow your instinct. The *Noble Hyacinth* is a mixture of pink and brown. It tells you to stop because an obstacle will be difficult to overcome: it's better to change your behavior or path."

Suddenly the butterflies became a swirling knot around her, forming a threatening cloud and falling upon the novice. Andraste began shouting and gesticulating, trying to escape them:

"Don't resist, otherwise they'll attack you." The priestess said quietly.

Andraste slowed her breathing and didn't move.

"Stretch out your arms."

The novice obeyed, feeling the butterflies land on her elegantly. Then, she felt tingling. It became more insistent. The butterflies were feeding on her blood! Cassandra watched silently. Andraste felt her will decline. With a gesture, she could easily destroy them! But she remembered her promise. *Never use magic to hurt a living being.* Cassandra's eyes gleamed with curiosity, but after a few minutes, she put an end to the torture with a quick movement, and the butterflies flew away.

"What do you think of the prophecies?

- I don't really know ... I wonder if they were placed end to end, if they'd even be consistent. And sometimes they seem more like poems than guidelines.

- That's an interesting point of view.

- Cassandra, I have a question. Are there spells or potions to cure madness?

- There's a truth potion, but nothing to cure madness. Why?

- Uh ... well I was wondering what the limits of magic were. Death obviously can't be undone, but I was wondering about ... madness. That's it."

Cassandra felt the gap widen between her and her novice. And that gripped her heart more than the fear that the prophecy might be fulfilled.

The guardian of the forest had accepted that she had a free afternoon, but not without difficulty. Why restrict her freedom all of the sudden?

The novice had drawn a circle and was now invoking the creature she wanted help from.

"Oh Longuins with fine hands, oh master singers, come to me now."

Kimpik, a Longuin the color of gold, approached with a coquettish air, his fingers smoothing his neck fur.

"May I offer you some tea? You can even try some of my pearls.

- I ... I thank you, Master Longuin, for coming. I need your help.

- Yes, I know. Call me Kimpik. I have what you need." He said, laughing.

Andraste was amazed at the ease with which he greeted her request. At the entrance of the burrow, she hesitated:

"I ... I don't know what to pay you, Kimpik. Well, I don't have much.

- I only ask for one thing: a strand of your hair."

He had a soft voice, as soft as the hair of his fur.

"A hair? Well ... that's fine."

Once settled inside the charming and warm burrow, Kimpik rummaged in a chest.

"Why do you live so close to the Azur? ... You don't mind?

- On the contrary. It's the least risky entrance to the forest for small creatures. Other creatures have entered the forest, little one," murmured Kimpik.

Andraste remained pensive, observing the den. Indeed, Cassandra wasn't able to say how many different magical races had entered the forest. The establishment of the Azur, the magical sphere, had been made in haste.

"But you should come and live near us in the forest!" cried Andraste. You'd be safer with Cassandra and me.

- It's better to stay here. Away from humans. What's done is done. Don't talk about the past."

He spoke with a natural authority, in a soft but firm voice. Kimpik waited for her to look at him again, and put a box on the table. A simple polished wooden box. The Longuin opened it smugly and Andraste looked inside. They were iridescent pearls of different colors.

"Choose one for yourself. Choose well, Andraste."

The novice chose a purple-colored pearl. She loved its soft, discreet color. In it, she saw green, iridescent reflections. What was this thing? Had they crushed a flower to blend with it... but blend

118

with what? She decided to ask the Longuin when she saw that he was watching, smiling. He encouraged her, laughing:

"Go ahead! Taste it! That's what you came for. To get answers to your questions!"

Andraste held it in her hands.

"I ... I just mainly came to see you for a potion. They say it's a weeping potion.

- Ho! ... Yes. A potion from the weeping tree. And how do you know that?

- I read it in a legend that talks about your people. Please, it's a secret that must remain between us. This is to help a friend ..."

The Longuin got up and came to what appeared to be the kitchen. He handed her a drinking gourd.

"It's a potion that restores the mind. It turns it right side up... or right side down..."

She thanked him, and before she could make a move, he cut a lock of her hair, and blew in her face:

"Libela uberul, excor piskim."

When she opened her eyes, she was standing at the edge of the river. The gourd and pearl in the palm of her hand confirmed that she wasn't dreaming. Yet she realized that she had lost sight of the entrance of Kimpik's borough ... She looked at the items in her hand for a moment. Why wait? She put the pearl in her mouth, but didn't feel anything special for the first few seconds. When she closed her eyes, she felt like she was taking off. She was the flower itself ... Or rather, the stem vibrating towards heaven, seeking warmth, and the petals of incomparable softness, fragile as paper. She had deep, fine and persistent roots, which allowed her to sway in the breeze, and to taste the slightly sweet rain. Her hair floated and danced around her head. Eyes still closed, she indulged in visions marching in her mind: first, the clouds, the rain, rocks shining in the downpour, and now the embers. Embers began to move. A creature appeared: it was a kind of eel, ears fanning out, with ruby eyes embedded in a triangular head. She waved her body made of pieces of the burning coals, and straightening her little head, speaking with a creamy voice:

"You have eyessss full of sssspecial magic, a very anc... sssiient magic..."

The eel nodded without blinking. Andraste asked:

"What is your name?

- My name is Pyrausssste.

- What magic are you talking about?

- The *Adrissskama*. Love, the desire that is dessssstined to you and that's sssstill hidden. An irrepressssible desire that will bind you two like a magnet.

- I don't understand. I'm not in love!

120

- You shall love, ssso much, desssssperately. It doessss not matter if you don't undersssstand. Very ssssoon you won't sssssee my face or remember me. "

Pyrauste disappeared into the flames and sparks. Suddenly, the flames burst and the elf was reaching for her... no! He was reaching for her medallion! He would brush it with his fingers as soon as Andraste pulled on the chain and fell backwards. The girl found herself lying on the floor and looking at the sky where Morphnée whirled. Doubt entered her mind. Would the elf really be her ally? And what if she'd misled him?

"So tell me what Cassandra taught you about crystals already?

- The imperial jasper for every day, celestite for contact with spiritual guides and protection during rituals, much like amazonite...

- I'm talking about their profound use. Their place in the universe and in this realm ... Our body has an invisible envelope that's imperceptible to the naked eye of most of the creatures. It's an invisible network, a web of channels spreading *Heka* everywhere. We have energy centers as hubs that distribute energy throughout. Through the forehead, throat, the center of the chest, the perineum, knees, ankles. These are the six seeds of light, the sources of growth for the body and our other envelope.

- What's the name of this envelope?

- *Yama*. But listen, this is key. The elements of any physical structure are created in the icy depths of space, long before they get down here to form flesh, bone, blood. The voice of the star resonates, literally, in our blood, and when we work to harmonize these stars, then we're in harmony with the cosmos.

- But Lyra, what does that have to do with the crystals?

- The crystals are stars, star pieces buried in the earth. By wearing them on your body or holding them in your hand, they resonate and help us to balance the *Heka* of all bodies."

Lyra was levitating stones and spiralling them around a large rock. Andraste was trying to listen carefully, but it was impossible to concentrate. Her thoughts wandered in the night sky in search of her falcon.

"I wanted to talk to you about something, Andraste. Don't invoke the Longuins. Too many races have suffered at the hands of humans. We cannot trust them.

- But I need to know who I am.

- Don't you think that you know yourself better and better?

- The more you teach me, the more questions I have, Lyra. How can I fulfill my destiny if I don't even know what I'm supposed to do?

- Learn. Obey. Be patient.

- You sound like Cassandra!"

Andraste turned and ran. Lyra didn't hold her back. Someone would tell her about the world of oblivion. She squeezed the gourd that Kimpik had given her in her hand, as if she were putting all her hope in it.

Andraste thought she'd hit the elf in the back of his head with her club, but the idiot had turned at the last moment. Tied to a chair, red faced, and haggard, the unconscious elf looked weathered. She grabbed him by the hair and threw his head back, forcing him to down the entire bottle. Seeing the state he was in, a little extra couldn't hurt. He had trouble swallowing, and Andraste thought he'd fallen asleep, his head flailing on his chest. His breathing returned to normal and he looked up, blinking, and clenching his fists. Stretching his legs, his eyes swept the room and fell on the novice. They looked at each other a moment. She cautiously reached out and gently laid her hand on his forehead. His body temperature was back to normal.

"I was crazy, but I wasn't going to bite you, you know.

- Do you remember your name?

- Lyander.

- Why are you in the forest?"

The elf was silent, but his muscles protruded under the cords to test their strength.

"I could ask you the same thing.

- I am novice to the service of the Caste of priests, under the tutelage of Cassandra, guardian of the forest of Etheldredre.

- Very impressive. Priests for me are nothing less than empty sages, terrible-smelling people who give blessings while spraying spittle everywhere. Would you untie me so that we can converse in a civilized manner? I feel stressed by the presence of these cords.

- Don't make fun of me. Answer my question and I'll untie you.

- I'm hunting a creature.

- But you were crazy. You attacked me.

- The hunting instinct never leaves an elf. We are born of the forest and the elements. They speak to us even in our dreams. And this creature is not good for the forest. Etheldrede told me, through my mind…however sick it was.

- What's this creature like?

- I did a stakeout in a tree. It's about two meters high, and it has claws, according fingerprints on the trunk. It attacks small magical creatures on the edge of the forest. And she only comes out at night.

- So you're here to chase after this creature...

- Ha, sorry there, but marriage is out of the question for now."

She slapped him hard enough that he felt the sting.

"What do you know about Anjara medallions?"

He seemed surprised.

"They're the most powerful relics, created not by priests, but by the Sabians. But it doesn't matter. Because they've supposedly all disappeared.

- But what were they used for?

- They protect the wearer. They allow him or her to pass the magical borders. It's probably the one you're wearing that allowed you to pass through the Azur."

Andraste opened her mouth in surprise.

"I was crazy, not stupid. Guard it carefully. The medallions don't fall into the hands of just anyone. It's chosen you somehow... "

Andraste continued her questioning suspiciously, remembering her vision.

"How did you pass through the Azur?

-       I benefited from a relic. You know what it is I guess ...
        ah yes, they're normally assigned to the priests, but I got
        my hands on one. I needed something to protect my
        body during transit. It's

become a form of currency in the other world. But, in magic, there's always a price to pay. And my mind didn't survive.

- Lyander ... But ... You're ... the son of Goiri. The one that never got to the battle! What happened to you? In the world of oblivion?"

He clenched his jaw and his eyes became black as ink.

"I was tortured by Faraoh. And now you're gonna ask me a list of my brothers, sister and female conquests, right?

- What's it like? The other world?"

Sensing his surprise, she added:

"I was born here. ... I'm an orphan. I was raised by the guardian of the forest."

Lyander gazed at her silently. He had no animosity in his eyes. Just a sincere curiosity. Andraste knelt carefully to untie his ropes. He stood up, his muscles relaxed, as he let his eyes rest on her. He was huge. He exceeded her height by two heads. With his broad shoulders and relaxed features, he wasn't the same person as before. Except for his proud and wild beauty that radiated from every pore of his skin.

"Why did you want to find the Temple of Hizaion?

- Because that's where my family is buried."

The girl bit her lip. They had more in common than she thought.

"Let's go hunting together. I know how to attract that creature. She feeds on *Heka*.

- I don't think so."

And before she could make a move, he brutally tied her down in the chair.

"I can help you find the creature! I know the forest.

- Me too, I grew up here. Before Faraoh."

Andraste felt anger rising. She had to find this creature that fed on her mother! She felt *Heka* discharge as her hands trembled.

"Hey Hoa Ladaksu!"

Nothing happened. The elf barely looked, preparing his quiver and arrows. He opened the door, when suddenly Andraste screamed with all her rage the formula:

"Hey Hoa Ladaksu!!!"

The impact was such that she fell forward, panting, seemingly broken into pieces. The elf was thrown back by an invisible barrier. The spell had worked.

- What do you think you're doing?

- You're condemned to remain locked up with me. You can't leave this house without me."

He began to swear:

"By Aum, I'll rip your head off!

- Elves, protectors of human, really?" Quipped Andraste, thinking of Lyra.

"Who are you talking to?

- Is it true? The elves are supposed to protect people?

- It's been a long time since things were like that."

In two steps he was on her. He seized her by the collar and pulled the chair.

"Break this spell.

- No.

- OK then."

He tied a rope to the chair, lifting his shoulders to open the window. Andraste held her breath: *he wouldn't* ... he threw the chair through the window. Andraste screamed at the top of her lungs, but the rope held on. She twirled slowly on it for a few seconds, a few meters from the ground. It wasn't fear, but anger that took hold in her. The elf cried,

"Break this spell!"

She replied angrily:

"No!!"

Lyander sighed. She added, shouting:

"No, because even if I wanted to undo it, I don't know how. I...
I don't know how to do undo it. But I know that if we go out together, you'll be freed."

128

Lyander hesitated, and nervously ran his hand through his hair. He refused to be responsible for her. Having to protect her. He climbed, slowly pulling the rope. The only way to keep her safe and sound was to keep himself away that he knew.

"Insolent! You break into my home, you stun me, you tie me up like a pig, you interrogate me with questions ... How old are you?

- I'm the age where one asks questions, not answers them... "

Lyander relaxed and placed her and her chair back on the floor: she was at most seventeen. She was trying to hide her innocence behind her wrinkled brow and serious expression, but the elf knew humans. She was still a child, impulsive, arrogant and fragile. Stepping back, he scratched the behind of his ear with a short dagger whose handle was finely carved. The elves were known for their good taste, skill, and art of exquisite finesse. He broke his cords, grabbing her by the neck, and lifted her from the ground. Pressing his face up to hers, he murmured:

"If ever you decide to throw another spell my way again, I'll use the dagger to cut your hair. And you'll look like a naughty stable boy."

Andraste felt his breath fresh and sweet. She felt the urge to lick his lips.

"I have one last question..."

Lyander clenched his fists, and placed it on the floor, slowly. As gently as he uttered his threat. She opened the door and looked back at the last minute:

"Aren't you going to thank me ... for the weeping tree potion?"

Lyander stifled a curse and a "thank you" as he followed her out.

Chapter 11

Lyander, hidden under a tree, watched the girl approach the foyer. She had to recover the cracked crystal from Cassandra. She couldn't use the talisman she'd given him. She left him and her wand outside for a moment. She climbed the tree and went through the window of her room. He was curious to see the priestess guarding the forest. She had brought the remains of his father and brother in the Temple. She deserved respect. He heard voices and sensed anxiety in the mind of the girl. The novice had been spot:

"You came back earlier from the forest didn't you?

- Yes ... but I'll go back. I would like to train a little extra tonight to make some more progress.

- Well ... good. Lots of tasks await you. I contacted the Council in your absence."

Andraste stopped dead in the doorway of her room.

"Your initiation will take place tomorrow evening."

The novice's heart beat faster. She was going to access the most secret knowledge in existence. She would have even more power. She'd no longer be a simple novice! She'd be an apprentice. All she had to do was stay alive for one more night. She went back to the elf, the crystal in her pocket. He saw her red cheeks and her eyes shining with excitement, despite the distance between them. Her whole being shimmered with anticipation.

Her life would begin at last! Her heart pounded, and she even laughed: she was to be initiated, then it would be the official ceremony. Given the exceptional situation, maybe she could even choose her specialty. Connector, scribe, psychic, healer, arshman, oracle ... Lyra suddenly spoke to her in her head:

"Andraste, don't go.

- But I don't see the risk, Lyra. I already hurt him once and Lyander is a seasoned fighter. I'll be safe.

- It is not a question of that Andraste ... I ... I'm beginning to grow weak, and I still have so much to teach you! Go back to the foyer."

Andraste stopped, breathless, and planted herself in the middle of the road.

"No—but what do you mean? Why are you weak?

- The forest has changed, like I've told you. There's a very menacing shadow being cast. And even if the forest remains protected, magic is dying. And me with it.

- This is the creature ... This is the Tengu, we're going to kill tonight!

- Andraste!" Lyra cried.

But Andraste had gone back, shaking her light hair behind her, closing her mind to the Daikini. Lyander greeted her by tightening his jaw. She pulled a small cloth out of her purse, which contained a small crystal.

"This is Cassandra's crystal. A crystal shard, at least. She hasn't used it for a long time!"

He nodded in response. They walked in silence, on tiptoe into the forest. Curiously, he liked to follow her steps with his own. He realized that she was the first human he'd encountered in decades. Elves didn't have the same needs as men. Food, nor sex had the same value or the same appeal. The elves nourished themselves on beauty and purity, in all its forms. She wasn't just beautiful: she was dangerous.

He followed her with a careful step, amusing himself by continually getting and closer to her without her noticing anything. She began to scrape the crystal with a small knife from out of her purse. The silver dust splashed ferns and nettles bushes along their way, while the girl and the forest were silent. It was an ominous melody, a ritual of destruction, which was preparing a strange night, the elf thought to himself.

They soon arrived at the clearing of the temple. Andraste beckoned him to point out the shadow of the temple, hidden from profane eyes with laurels and lime trees. He ran for a moment along the space littered with upright stones, engraved with ancient texts. Her heart beat wildly. His family, his brothers, his lineage, were all reposed there. He advanced to the middle of the clearing. He refused to let her see his tears. He needed to be alone. Suddenly, the attack was on.

The Tengu screamed and dove on him. He struck him in the chest and scooped him into the air. Andraste shot him with her sling: the stone made contact with the Tengu's wing, but barely slowed his pace. Lyander smelled the Tengu's foul breath against his face.

"You have a brave heart. But do I feel it accelerating?"

The Tengu let go above the pyramid. He didn't have time to draw his dagger from his boot. The elf almost impaled himself on the top of the pyramid. He gripped as best he could on the slippery rocks covered with moss. When he saw the creature standing in front of Andraste, his blood ran cold and he fell on the back of Hiero. Hiero stepped back, breaking the sacred tablets in his path. This time, it was Andraste that grazed the Tengu's leg passing under his wing. She understood what had to be done.

They rushed into the temple through the door Lyander had opened. They dashed inside without a word, as far as they could. Andraste missed her Daikini, but Lyra was nowhere to be found.

They came to a large room where an empty and dusty fountain adorned with silent sculptures waited for them. They couldn't stay. They needed a plan.

"I'll attract him. I'm fair game for him, and he wants my medallion. You attack from behind near his head, and attack him as soon as the Tengu moves. Go for the ears. They're the weak spot. Put your index finger in them to keep them open, or else they'll close for his own protection. I'll be back in a few minutes."

Andraste took a tunnel on the left, going back into the underground of the temple. Lyander fumed: these humans! He hated them and their arrogance! She had just given him orders and

134

made decisions alone. She was putting him in danger, her in danger! He leaned back where he was still covered by shadows.

"Prince Lyander ... of the City of Samatya ..."

The elf heard claws scraping the ground, while the silky voice hissed.

"The last heir of the house of Goiri ... A guardian without his flock ...

- You're not the one we're looking for...

- But I'm looking for you. Where is she?

- She fled from your rat face."

Andraste darted out from the tunnel while a cry pierced the walls. The monster had once again attacked. She hadn't gone very far, and had retraced her steps when she heard her wheezing. She stood behind the creature, clinging to the bones of its wing. But she couldn't climb over it to reach the creature's ears. She planted the dagger in her left hand below his shoulder blade and climbed on his back. In a split second, she pressed her index finger in the Tengu's ear. Hiero screamed, arched, and jumped, attempting to throw her off. But the creature was trapped in the cramped room. He screamed again, deafening the room with his cries, as Andraste had predicted. The only issue now was the tunnels. Andraste saw the elf who used his combat blades to lacerate the torso and arms of the creature. She felt the Tengu weaken. She pulled the dagger out of its shoulder blade and tried to apply it against the monster's throat. But he was faster than her, and took advantage of her split-second of inattention, grabbing her by the hair and throwing her against the wall. Andraste gasped. She had felt the shock vibrate through her body, all the way to her rib cage. The creature then grabbed the elf by the throat and slammed him against the wall. Andraste, in a last effort, grabbed the dagger lying on the floor under the Tengu's legs.

"No!"

Lyander stopped her. They needed to stall.

"No, I need the creature living.

Hiero, at these words, still holding Lyander in his claws, met his face with its purulent, wet, black eyes.

"Need?

- Faraoh has called you back. Your master calls you.

- Tsssss Faraoh, "my master" calling me ... Well, well ... Would he perhaps be in need of my help again?

- I am here to take you to him. Safe and sound."

Hiero released the elf, but stood nearby watching his movements.

"Really?

- You're the only monster housed in the forest.

- Really?"

Hiero's voice suddenly sounded strange. The Tengu turned its head and looked at Andraste, smiling mischievously.

"Your father didn't teach you the science of *Heka* ... This kid is who you're looking for.

136

Andraste struggled to catch her breath. Hiero was on her in seconds, taking her medallion. With a hand on her medallion, Hiero stared into her eyes, and grabbed her by the throat.

Lyander came to his senses and drew his last blade in his ribs. But Hiero ordered him:

"Look, Prince Lyander!"

Andraste, immobilized, tried to resist the taste in her mouth. A call that rose deep from within her insides. A call convened by contact with Hiero's skin. A thirst for blood. Not just any blood. A pain shot through her bones, then her skull. Andraste's transformation began. Lyander, amazed, saw the girl's eyes shine with a special glow, a glow that he began to recognize. They turned black ringed with blue. Suddenly, black, blue streaks, dug their way under her skin, like drought-crackled earth. It was obvious her transformation was causing her to suffer. When her nostrils became two slots, the girl opened her mouth and let out a terrible scream tearing the foundations of the earth. She seemed to release anger, hatred, hunger and suffering. It was a complaint, a howl to death no creature had ever unleased on the lands of Hizaion. Lyander saw her black tongue, amidst toothy, purplish saliva, which contrasted with her now cadaver-like skin. Andraste no longer thought; she felt all her hair stand on end. Her body became steel, and arched under the pressure of Tengu's fingers. Her legs were taken by uncontrollable convulsions, and she felt her feet stretch and her nails bleed into her shoes. When she looked at her fingers grasping her opponent, she saw her cracked purple skin, and her monstrous and powerful claws. Hiero grinned and grabbed Andraste by her hair and lifted her from the ground like a miserable, disjointed puppet. Lyander then grabbed the dagger from the ground and planted it between the Tengu's shoulder blades.

Hiero produced a hoarse cry, releasing Andraste to the floor. She exchanged a glance with Lyander, then threw herself under the body of the monster out of this mess where she had thrown herself.

The elf ran for hours, crying out. He shut the door of the temple of the flat and high stone. He hoped that Hiero had lost enough blood to remain trapped inside. Lyander reflected intensely, catching his breath. Suddenly, Lyra spoke to him in his mind, slipping him the right words. He left swiftly.

Andraste, kneeling, having regained her human form, was trying to put her hands on the roses that bloomed near the lake. She sang, sobbing, still reeling from what had happened, while he watched. The elf was distraught, torn. He scrutinized her trembling silhouette without being able to fathom it. How was it possible? What magic had been present at her birth? Was she the reincarnation of a demon from the old days? He had to face the truth, the girl disturbed him. And it was not her monstrosity that made her so mysterious.

Andraste hummed, trembling, cold, and frightened. She was crying watching the roses bloom, from the depths of the earth to the surface. She sang:

"Dana, shining star

God is revealed through you,

Mother, the more I see you, the more I find you beautiful,

And I just put my heart on your altar,

Make it pure in your eyes, give me my innocence,

Faith, charity, sublime hope,

Meanwhile, Dana, mother of all the broken-hearted,

Those that fate has cursed

Keep me heart child-like,

Pure and transparent as your fountain,

Give me a great and indomitable heart,

Loyal, generous, gentle, humble"

Under her voice, the roses stirred gently under her charm. But when the girl approached them with her hands, they retreated, as if they were injured. The more Andraste made efforts to contain the rage and despair that rose in her, the more the roses, twisted, sagged, and emptied themselves of their juice, their *Heka*. Andraste heard movement behind her. When she turned, Lyander saw her skin paler than ever, as her eyes became purple, staring at him. Was it the evil itself which took possession of her, or the exhaustion of the fight against this part of herself? The elf noticed that the Anjara medallion glowing an ominous glow. Andraste said, in a broken voice:

"It's me isn't it? When I don't transform myself, the forest is injured, it's the forest which is changing, dying..."

She was crying. The roses fell to the ground now.

"You're going to kill me, aren't you?

- No, no. Protect you. I want to protect you.

- Then help me. I'm not bad. I ... I want to get rid of this beast in me.

- I know." He let himself kneel down on the ground beside her.

He took her in his arms, and she leaned against him, inhaling his fragrance. Lyra appeared in the dew. Her handsome face veiled sadness, and she spoke softly:

"I tried to protect you...

- Everyone wants to protect me, but everyone lies to me or hides the truth!"

Andraste had recovered, and she was furious. She stared at the elf with angry black eyes. He too came from another world, and he was an ally of Faraoh. A traitor! Lyra resumed, imploring:

"I tried to extricate you: I thought maybe you were possessed in the beginning. But it's something else. It's not magic. It's your medallion that prevents you from transforming, but I don't know why. This thing, who lives in you, it comes from the other world. The world of oblivion.

-And I come from the other world..." said Andraste in a broken voice.

If magic and spells could do nothing for her, she was doomed. Lyra sighed. She became so weak that her image vanished. Andraste, with her head down, was thinking intensely. Her heart was beating fast as always, and her mind was restless. Fresh tears rolled down his cheeks, as the horrible truth emerged in her mind. The evidence of her true nature was revealed:

"The forest is dying. Lyra ... you're dying because of me ... She said in a hoarse voice.

- Your two natures can no longer live together, yes. But don't think that. You're going to be initiated, and you'll be charged with a mission by the Council. And we need you to have faith, and courage not to sink into hatred, resentment, or fear. Courage and faith Andraste. The Anjara medallion will protect you, but it can also reveal your different nature, the beast in you.

- But how is that possible? What am I?"

The girl felt abandoned, lost. She had seen the body, so she had had a mother. She was human, dammit, it had to be a mistake!

"You were born human, but something happened before you were born.

- But how does the Tengu know more about my origins than me?

- I ... "

Lyra sighed, and became increasingly pale. Andraste screamed the name of the Daikini to get her attention. She needed answers too: they weren't just impertinent questions or curiosity. It was her life, her future. This was who she really was. Lyander stepped forward and recited a prayer in an unknown language, raising a ring she hadn't noticed. And slowly, his ring glowed. Gradually, as the light of the Daikini was waning, the ring became become brighter, glowing.

"Who are you?" Asked Andraste in a sigh. She was exhausted, tired of the lies and secrets. She was sad, scared, and angry.

"I am your friend, your ally.

- "Prince Lyander?" Traitor! Double traitor who was supposed to protect the royal family." She suddenly sneered harshly.

She wanted to hurt him. She wanted him to have it as bad as she did. He gritted his teeth. His words were also a stinging slap. The face of the girl, however, was back to normal, reflecting sadness. It was, after all, a good sign he thought.

"Your protector is safe in my ring. Its essence is safe and sound, but we must hurry. Let's bring her home to your guardian. Maybe she can treat her."

Without a word, Andraste turned away from the evil eye, and took the way home without looking back, measuring her steps. Lyander followed her without a word, like a shadow of herself. Or perhaps he had already become a shadow a long time ago.

Cassandra reacted as she always did when faced with the unexpected: coldly and rationally. An elf, and a Daikini were in Etheldrede without her knowledge. Worse, her pupil had deliberately concealed this information. Cassandra didn't even look at Andraste. It was a betrayal. The healer priestess went for celestite crystals on the shelves, and placed them in a triangle on the cleared kitchen table. She placed Lyander's ring in the center and repeated the same prayer as the elf. Was it an elven spell? Or that of the Sages, and their lost language? Andraste had never heard Cassandra perform a spell in that language. Lyra appeared amidst the glow of the celestite.

"I'm Cassandra, healer and Etheldrede priestess. Who are you?

- Lyra, Daikini princess, daughter of Albéron. The last of the Daikini people, remaining to protect this child. I've been here since her birth."

Cassandra's eyes narrowed. So it was she who had deposited the child.

"Where's her mother?

- She died during childbirth. I don't know who she was.

- What's happening to you?

    - The forest is dying, and me with it."

The tension in the room was palpable. The sinister crack of burning logs punctuated the dialogue between the two women. Fire sheaves shone nervously.

"Why is the forest dying?

- Because of the Destroyer prophecy. It is coming to fruition.

- Nobody knows the whole prophecy.

- It doesn't matter. The priests didn't anticipate the last oracle to respond.

- Tell me. Tell me the whole prophecy. The full text. We need it. To prepare for the future!

- The future no longer belongs to you. You already had the cards in hand the last time. Look what the certainties of the priests did to Hizaion and the sanctuary of Etheldrede!

- We misread the signs...

-Your pride and weakness led the priestly caste, the men, and magical creatures of the world of Hizaion to their end. Prophecies and oracles are made for the weak who are afraid of the future."

Andraste had never heard so much harshness in Lyra's voice.

" Look there! You wait for years to initiate her even though she represents the hope of the world Hizaion.

- She's ... she's only a child.

- You know perfectly well that she was never just a child."

Lyra then turned her gaze to Andraste and pointed to the parchment she was still holding at her side.

"The revelation that comes can be interpreted in different lights. The Destroyer prophecy was made about her well before the arrival of Faraoh. But the real question that should occupy your thoughts, Cassandra, is your actions: they are our abyss or our salvation. Yes there is a destiny, a prophecy, but we perceive only bits as fate changes, like pieces on a chessboard. It readjusts itself. We outline the plan, and we must do what is right. Thus, destiny will be fulfilled. My people left the forest years ago. The fate of Etheldrede is now in your hands, Cassandra. Farewell, Andraste, keep me in your heart. As a sister.

- Lyra ..."Andraste felt her heart break.

The Daikini smiled. Andraste thought she saw a tear in her eye. Could a Daikini, a being so perfect and beautiful, really die?

"When you're the world of oblivion ... Be flexible like a reed faced with the unexpected. Be like the original algae with its deep roots and millions of years of secrets and tenacity. Flexible and intuitive. Follow the currents. Be discreet. Don't seek power. And agree to not know everything. Goodbye Etheldrede, farewell Onesimus, Father, I'll soon be joining our ancestors…"

Andraste felt like she was in a nightmare. Her throat tightened, while they smiled sadly. It was a silent farewell, painful and unfair like all farewells. Lyra disappeared like a smile evaporated into the air, while dawn pierced the window panes of the house and greeted the death of the last Daikini of Etheldrede.

Three knocks then sounded. Cassandra, haggard, stepped back from the table searching for the origin of the noise. Suddenly, she turned and ran towards her seat. She carefully took out a wooden chest, which was surprisingly simple.

"The Sages, the priests ... They've arrived sooner than expected!

- What? But ...

- We will discuss your betrayal later, Andraste. Run and prepare their rooms."

Andraste exchanged an indecipherable glance with Lyander then turned to go upstairs. She was opening the shutters when he appeared behind her, without a sound.

Chapitre 12

Lyander's lips were dry like sand.

"I can explain everything you want know.

- I don't want to hear anything from the mouth of a traitor.

- I'm not a traitor. Yes, I was sent to bring a creature that had escaped Faraoh. But I wouldn't have done it... I tried to kill you, remember?

- Shut up! Go away! I don't want Cassandra hear you!

- I would never hurt you. I cannot hurt you. Believe that much. »

Andraste felt herself waver: These translucent blue eyes pierced her innermost feelings. She was ashamed of having transformed in front of him. What would he think of her now? He must find her repugnant. She looked up bravely:

"You won't bring me back to him. I was born here, I belong to Etheldrede.

- Good. Stay here with me in Etheldrede. We'll find a way. Even better, as the Caste wouldn't want you as a priestess. I'll find a solution."

He approached slowly, the strands of his hair stuck to his

forehead, blocking his beautiful but tormented features. They had shared so little together, but how intense it was. They belonged to the same world, the old world, and were carved from the same stone. Banished and cursed. He took her hand and gently placed his face in her palm. Andraste leaned back, closing her eyes. Behind those crazy eyes, she had always felt and feared that sweetness.

"I will never betray because I cannot betray what I...

- What are you doing here?" Rang the dry voice of Cassandra behind him.

The Andraste's tutor stood in the doorway and stared furiously at Lyander

"Andraste, I need your help to prepare for their arrival. Take the sacred oil of Frankincense."

Andraste slipped gently from his side. The elf felt her heart beating in the veins of the hand that he'd just released. A heart never lied. He heard Andraste slowly climb down the stairs to try to listen to the conversation that followed. Left alone, he and Cassandra surveyed each other for a moment.

"What's an elf doing in the forest of Etheldrede?

- I wanted to honor my ancestors buried in the first temple.

- Did you find them?

- Yes. Thank you. With the help of your novice.

- She now knows the forest better than me."

He walked over to Cassandra. The guardian of the forest thought fleetingly back to Goiri and his last words. Was he the son, guilty of perjury, who abandoned his own and had never came?

"Good. I'll leave you to your tasks now, my lady. "

She stood aside to let him pass. By the time he left, she asked him:

"What's it like? Outside?

- Worse than you could ever imagine." He let slip, head bowed.

Andraste waited for Cassandra outside the house and admired the priestess's set-up. Seven Obsidian disks hung from hemp ropes of seven oaks, identifying the clearing before the house. How was it possible that she had never seen these trees form such a perfect circle?

Lyander came to her side and put a hand on her shoulder, looked into her eyes for just a moment, then going on his way. Andraste reflects. She still blamed him, even if he was allied with the dark side. With Faraoh. How was that possible ... He was so noble. An elf. A veteran of the Battle of Goiri. Cassandra pulled her out of her thoughts, and snapped in a harsh voice.

"Smear each disc with sacred oil. In silence. Even your thoughts must be silent."

Andraste bit her lip, looking down at her shoes. Would she forgive her someday?

The girl began around the oak trees, where the first disk hung. She observed it, black, opaque, full, and dipped her fingers in lavender oil to purify it. Her gaze was aloof as she expunged any entity that could be hiding within it, by drawing a cross on it with her finger. *Spirit incarnated though this material.* She'd made this cross sign on her neuralgic points every morning since Lyra taught her. She didn't care what Cassandra thought about it, the girl was crying in her heart, and wanted to make a final tribute to her patron, her mentor...

Then it was frankincense: Andraste coated all discs, thus increasing their magical power.

Cassandra beckoned her to join her at the center of the circle. Andraste then turned to notice that she had abandoned her dark red wool dress for a traditional priestess outfit. White, long, sewn with silver arabesques, the dress of the priestess and healer revived the glory of the old days. Could it be that her generation would really save the world? What was this prophecy of which Lyra and Cassandra had spoken?

Cassandra opened a chest at her feet: she took out a golden bowl, and a little heavy stick whose handle was made of wrapped hemp. She held the bowl in the palm of her left hand up to her chest, arms extended from her body, and knocked the bowl once with the stick. A great wind arose, gently at first, then powerfully. The light changed, the clouds darkened. The air became almost stormy. Cassandra knocked the bowl again. A tension between air, wind, atmosphere, and earth was taking place. At one point, the young novice thought she was hallucinating: microscopic particles remained in suspension. She thought they were raindrops, but upon closer look, they didn't move. Instead, they were sustained and shimmered as if fighting against gravity. Cassandra knocked the bowl then a third time. The storm tore the air. The particles assembled and became so bright it that it blinded the priestess and the novice, who protected her instinctively. It lasted a fraction of a second, but Andraste was giddy. She lowered her arm and blinked a few seconds ... Three silhouettes, no. Nine silhouettes stood out now, while the bowl still ringing. The wind calmed, stopped, and the silhouettes materialized. The Council was there. Two priests. Four Sage leaders. Three teenagers, a girl and two boys stood behind them, with a somewhat reassured air. Probably novices.

Andraste had never read a description of the Board members, the Sages. She knew they were four, four Elders with immense knowledge, directing the priestly caste. They had once been the preferred partner of King. Cassandra stepped forward and greeted them in the customary way.

"*Nalada Shunga*. Welcome all to the forest of Etheldrede."

They looked exhausted. Andraste remotely sensed that their bodies were hardened by the experience of travel, and their minds still foggy. Aman, appearing to be the oldest, came forward, one hand clutching his stick topped with a raven, the other on his heart. He opened the palm of his hand and held it open, his elbow slightly bent. It was a solemn salute for a seemingly paunchy and friendly man. Wyre, a woman of indefinable age, had short hair and deep black eyes surrounded by grooves. She was beautiful, with a special kind of femininity, and dressed all in white. She was the essence of gentleness, humility and intransigence. Kunrun was tall, thin, and dark-skinned, with dry eyes and a closed jaw. He had his own beauty, an ascetic beauty, thought Andraste. But it was the last member of the Council who intrigued her. He looked wild, dressed in black and dark green, unlike the others. He had to be a healer because of the satchel at his side, which usually held roots and dried leaves. A small knife was slipped into his belt. He looked more like a master poisoner from the lowlands than a healer. While Aman and Cassandra exchanged pleasantries, Agaric felt the eyes of Andraste over him and stared back at her: he looked like a wolf.

The three novices trembled with cold now: where did they come from? Was it the shock of the trip? There was a girl whose hair was arranged in a coil of white-striped hemp. Her frail body was wrapped up in a dark wool coat while she kept her pale face leaning forward, trying to concentrate all her body heat inside. Her lips murmured an inaudible prayer. Was that what she'd look like? Andraste felt uncomfortable in her new dress made from old pieces of Cassandra's dresses, and caked-on grime that had certainly invaded her face after the night she had spent.

"Tonight?!" Cassandra gasped. She looked dazed at the four Sages, dazed.

"But...

- Time is running out, we must return to our posts, Cassandra. We must find and train other novices. It's a miracle to have found and trained Beeja, Hal, and Dehir in so little time.

- Yes, I'm surprised ... Where are they from?

- Rosendal, and Braque. Rosendal remains the bastion of our resistance, but Aygulf fears *arshman* plaguing the forest and frightening the population. As for me, I deal with the Senate. We must leave tomorrow morning.

- With the Senate? V ... very well, Master.

- Agaric, Wyre and Kunrun will lead the novices in the forest for the first part of the initiation, then they'll be back tonight for the inauguration."

With that, Aman and the other Sages turned away, and exchanged a few whispered words. Aygulf quickly came towards Cassandra to hug her, smiling. A great complicity united them, it was obvious. If Andraste knew what it was, she would have said it was a filial-type love. She knew Aygulf was Cassandra's tutor. Ferens was more involved in the development of educational programs. He was appreciated for his energetic personality and had played a role in the negotiations between the Priestly caste and royalty. He sized up Andraste from top to bottom: just as an insect waiting to crush its prey. She stared at him viciously in his eyes, wanting to crucify him on the spot by the sheer force of his pupils. She felt that the war for her place in the Caste was already beginning.

"Cassandra, could your student prepare a meal for the day? We need to something to sustain ourselves after an intense trip."

Cassandra released the Aygulf's embrace and smoothed her dress:

"Andraste, go set-up the novices in your room, and ask them to help you prepare meals. Something rich and filling. You know what to do."

Andraste turned to head back towards the foyer. The enthusiasm for her initiation had fallen to after being met with so little kindness. What information had Cassandra sent to the Council of Elders? From the corner of her eyes, the girl saw Cassandra speak quietly with the three Elders and the two priests. Aman stared at Wyre, listening carefully to Cassandra's words. Andraste turned away but felt all eyes on her neck. She had always tried to prove to Cassandra that she was at the height of the priestess vocation. But it was not Cassandra who had the power of life and death over her fate: it was the Council. The girl felt the beating of her heart accelerate. How could she convince the Caste to accept her?

Inside, the priests were set-up in the upstairs bedrooms. They were small individual rooms, but clear, airy, and warm at night by the column of the house's central chimney. She went into the kitchen, gathering the herbs, spices and ingredients she needed for the recipe, and put them on the table. Suddenly Andraste's pulse skipped a beat when she heard footsteps, just above, in her room. She dropped everything and ran up the stairs four at a time: she came face to face with Aman coming out of her room. He held Andraste's notebook, her personal spell book. All of her notes from her sessions with not only Cassandra, but Lyra as well. With her senses alert, she tried to display her surprise and a serene demeanour.

"Master, forgive me, if I'd known you wanted to see my room I would have arranged it."

- I just got a bit confused…Andraste, is it?

- Yes, Master."

Andraste let her voice flow docility. She had to recover her journal at any cost.

"Master, I wish to have my journal back, I'd like to review it before tonight. I've awaited your arrival for so long. I would hate to forget any of my questions."

It was better to use this argument. A novice, an apprentice, appealing to a priest belonged to the Caste. He'd made vows of chastity and obedience, but he'd also given up contradicting orders, or having a private life. Aman squinted at the details of Andraste's features, as if dissecting her.

"I am very surprised that you still have questions after such an intensive and sharp training."

She felt sweat beading in the hollow of her back. The apparent benevolent and sweet Aman was hiding something. The girl then noticed the pink spots dotting his skin, and his puffy lips moistened regularly that before long sentences. A small smile played at the corners of his mouth.

"You won't need it tonight. Listen with your heart and let the questions flow from your mind. I'll study it."

Andraste hung a smile on her face, and held back the urge to bludgeon his face with her fist. The wrinkles that lined the Sage's face crinkled further.

«Do you have something to add, little one?

- Don't call me little." Murmured Andraste.

Her words cut his smile abruptly. She felt anger welling up inside her. Who does he think he is? He entered her room, he stole her diary, her most intimate possession, and she had to be respectful and courteous to him. She felt her blood boil. What kind of Sage was he?

Hal, Beeja, and Dehir came out of their room at the same time. Had they heard everything?

"Let's prepare the meal," she said casually. She capitulated, but only for the moment. Aman, slipping Andraste a lingering stare, slid her journal in his inside pocket, mounting the stairs.

Left alone, she rushed to her room and knelt to feel under the mattress. Lyander's dagger was still there. Praise be to Dana! The presence of the Sages, the two priests and three novices complicated her secrets. She resolved to go talk to Cassandra about her notebook. Aman while the Master, was not her protector. She was accountable to Cassandra.

"What are you looking for?" Rang a voice softly behind her.

It was Beeja, frail, pale and shy. She looked like a dove, thought Andraste. She would not survive the initiation, she thought. She was too frail, and she seemed so unsure of herself. Andraste rose nonchalantly:

"Master Aman took what I value most.

- Something more precious than your medallion?"

Andraste reached for the chain. Her pendant had slipped out of her shirt while she was bending under the bed.

"I..."

Beeja giggled:

'Oh don't worry, I won't say a word. The design is pretty. Where did you borrow it?

- It's a gift from my mother. She died giving birth to me."

The little novice turned crimson in her white cap and bit her lower lip.

"Oh," she said, in one breath.

Andraste smiled and took her by the arm, dragging her down the stairs. She didn't want to dwell on it. It was almost the middle of the morning and they still had to prepare a meal before their test in the forest.

The two boys had set the table while the priests were behind the house, sitting on rocks. Was it a dream? Andraste felt that Lyra and her teachings were so far away. Today she was going to prove herself in the eyes of the Council who would accept or reject her....

She asked Hal to cut the turnips and Dehir scrape the skin of the sweet potatoes. While Beeja cooked black lentils with raisins, Andraste prepared the mixture of spices that would be mixed with crumbs, goat cheese thyme, chervil, coriander, plus salt and pepper. They had to prepare the dishes twice because they didn't have a large enough pan. It was the first time they'd opened their home to seventeen people... tried to eavesdrop, but she couldn't understand the conversations of the priests outside. They had cleverly placed themselves in the direction of the wind.

Agaric caught the young novice's eye through the window. He was holding a book in his hands. Andraste recognized the dark green binding: it was a potions book, including the recipe for mordenite, made from khemeia, a black, carbon powder of the gods. What a strange, dark and enigmatic character. How old could he be?

Hal, who'd finished, approached the library while whistling and scanning the bindings. He was a handsome young man, with youthful, unbridled freshness: tall, blonde, with lofty traits, he had an almost feminine grace. Yet women liked him, it was obvious. He enjoyed teasing Beeja, who blushed, scurrying away and giggling. He had a charming smile and Andraste couldn't help but compare it to the elf. Had he once looked like this young man from a good family? She was certainly surprised at the docility with which he participated in the kitchen. It was like a game for him, as if he wasn't concerned. Dehir, meanwhile, was a stocky boy. Black curls framed his impassive and secretive face. He had to be from the tribe of Hounds, the humans originally living in the forest.

The priests finally returned for lunch. Exceptionally, they took the meal together, but in silence. Andraste remained deep in thought, and tasted the goat cheese she had soaked a few minutes in the lemon juice. This dish was a success, melty and savory for the taste buds. It would keep them throughout the afternoon. Her intuition told her that they would push their initiation to the point of hunger. She could hold out, but she was worried about Beeja. Her initial suspicion out of the way, Andraste was happy to know that she was not alone. Their missions would surely intersect ... Without a word, Agaric rose once he was finished eating, grabbing his leather bag, polished by the years, and slinging it on his shoulder. The novices cleaned the table while the priests and Sages returned outside. Cassandra held Andraste back when the rest of the novices had gone.

"It's not really a test, you know. This is a sensitivity test to detect your skills, your qualities. Trust, Andraste, trust.

- I'm sorry I hid things from you, Cassandra ... I don't know why I did that.. I wanted to protect them. It was my little world. My family...

- I believe, contrary to Lyra, that there is a child in you. Stubborn, talented and fragile. But she's there, behind your maturity and your undeniable qualities as a priestess.

Andraste felt her chest warm. It was one of the nicest compliments Cassandra had ever given her. Better still, it renewed her confidence. The girl smiled, gratefully, and went off with a lighter heart. She would honor her two protectors.

"Tonight will be the real test..." Cassandra sighed.

Agaric rose from the stone where he sat, watching Andraste and her guardian. His bushy eyebrows framed a whittled face. He had a thin nose and indiscernible nostrils that fell into a thick beard. Andraste could make out thin lips accustomed to mumble incantations without a sound. He got up without a word when the girl approached their group, and went towards the forest. Wyre and Kunrun brought up the rear. Andraste felt new strength running through her veins. She had waited for this moment her entire childhood. She was running to prove to the sages that she was capable. She was ready.

They went out into the river, then crossed the field. The sun was beating down on their necks but Andraste loved that feeling. The three novices unaccustomed to northern climate and this season struggled. They were looking for where best to place their feet to avoid ferns, nettles and other secrets of nature. Hal finally let Andraste pass him, pouting haughtily and clenching his jaw, falling into exact step with her. Agaric and the two Sages apparently did not need to look at the ground: was it the grass or

Heka guiding their path? Agaric cut through the air and the tall grass with ease.

They finally arrived at the edge of the forest, but branched off to the south. They skirted, beeches, oaks and wild roses. Agaric's guttural voice was heard for the first time, asking Dehir the names of the plants they encountered throughout their pilgrimage. The boy knew by heart their applications, their poultices, and their magic powers, but it was much more difficult for him to recognize them. He answered all despite some hesitation and looks distraught to other novices. Beeja let himself overcome by anxiety. Suddenly, Agaric went into the forest. Andraste knew little about this part of the territory of Eheldrede. They walked in silence for a while. Suddenly, the guttural voice of Agaric said:

"Young Hal!"

He jumped up like a young goat to join the sage.

"The power of prayer?"

Hal remained silent. He was not expecting a question on this subject!

"It is an expression of hope, but also the repetition of words uttered for centuries ... And ... these words through being repeated take power. Almost as much as thought. Prayer indeed is the union of words and thought ... and the image that forms in the mind elsewhere."

It was a pretty good explanation, thought Andraste. But it lacked heart.

"Heart ..." growled agaric in a spanning tree. Andraste swallowed. Was he a telepath?

"It's an expression from the heart. This is an alchemy of mind that actually takes power with words and images. But what is the final ingredient, Andraste?"

She took a moment to think. The three novices looking at her looked worried and dumbfounded. How could she take her time to respond?

Agaric stopped and turned to her. With all eyes on the ground, Andraste carefully selected every word she uttered. She wanted to give a sober and compelling answer.

"The *Heka* is already there, ready to be used. It takes faith, and a strong desire to propel it into reality. An irrepressible desire. Prayer moves outward; it must be an anchor to give it more force. Faith enables this anchor ... and thus a concentration of *Heka*."

Agaric pondered a few moments. Andraste had to resolve to face up to him and let him plunge his irises in hers. It wasn't unpleasant. Just unusual for the girl.

"And what is the key formula for every prayer?

- I am. But it's not a prayer. It is an incantation.

162

- And the difference between an incantation and invocation, dear Beeja?"

The frail novice with black eyes blinked and said softly:

"The incantation is sufficient in itself. The invocation requests the assistance of an entity.

- By Hul, this is a class we haven't seen in years."

Wyre said clearly, singing the compliment to lighten the mood. The novices, authorized to smile, relaxed a little.

"Make a fire. Together."

The three novices divided the tasks according to their physiques. Hal went to look for wood with Dehir, while Beeja gathered twigs to start the fire. Andraste cleaned the circular space. Sticks, stones, everything was organized to make an undergrowth where they left off, a small clearing. Agaric was still watching Andraste. His eyes shone in the darkness of the woods. What he mumbled under his beard made her freeze on the spot:

"Destroyer..."

Chapter 13

Andraste stopped dead in her tracks. Had she heard right?

"We're going to give everyone a lesson," said Kunrun approaching them, in a measured voice.

"Then we'll meditate, but each at our individual locations—united in thought."

The Sage, his face tanned and his eyes elongated, sat wrapped up in his coat. Dehir drank in his words.

"You must live by your hands, have pride in your work, and you must demonstrate the skills you'll offer to the community. You will provide a service to the community. Sometimes you'll eat on the floor, sometimes you'll sleep on the floor, you'll work on the floor. There aren't contracts in the caste—no written contracts, at least. You'll engage in an endless path. A life-long mission. Ten years, twenty years ... time doesn't exist. And no one receives any money. If you come for the money and the glory, you don't belong with us. You'll come for the work, the abnegation, and the challenge. With us, you'll look for new paths. It's thought that's the foundation of everything, before any action. Failure does not matter. You'll simply start over. Just as this plant dies in winter and blooms in spring, you, like the plant, you will spread your own seeds and be reborn. You'll be as a much a student as a teacher. We do not issue certificates. You will be certified by the experience and by the community you serve. You do not need a paper on the wall to prove that you are priests. You'll learn to listen more, and you'll continue learning to listen, without end. You'll learn to look for solutions within. "

Kunrun spoke with an enthusiastic and convincing voice. Wyre stepped forward and covered her head, rocking back and forth a few minutes, closing her eyes, letting a melodious voice escape. The three novices listened, mesmerized. She sang of Dana, the earth, the first Sabians, demi-gods who had shared their knowledge with humans and magical creatures. Andraste savored the sweet melody in the darkness of the forest, which had closed in on them like a cocoon. Wyre finished her song. Andraste, in a daze, waited for her to start again. Hal listened, hazily and delighted in the sounds, devouring her with his eyes as if she was the goddess herself. They let all the silence settle in and listen to the melody of the logs crunching in the fire. Fireside, Agaric spoke in a firm and soft voice.

"This initiation isn't only tests, or even private lessons: through my questions, I gave you things you have to work on. You're still missing pieces of the puzzle. But know one thing: you know nothing. Make this phrase your prayer, a battle cry against the Shadow. *I know that I know nothing.* Repeat this to yourself and you will remain open, available, and ready to learn, even from the Shadow. You must hold on to it all your life. This will become your master. "

With that, Agaric got up and went to curl up against the roots of an oak. One might say he looked like a calm effigy lying amidst of nest of snakes.

Everyone retired to a corner which suited him. Andraste went off even further. She needed space to rest and meditate. The events of the recent days had left her exhausted. Wyre's singing had provoked waves of emotion in her, to the point of being uncontrollable. Her mother, her transformation, the death of Lyra, Lyander ... All of it tossed around in her head. What would become of her?

Her head resting against a pile of dead leaves, she dozed on the floor, too tired to care about anyone else. Suddenly, a hand closed on her mouth. Lyander had slipped behind her. She gave him a nudge, dissatisfied. But he insisted and took her by the hand to lead her even further, far from the eyes and sharpened ears of the Sages.

"What are you doing here? Are you trying to ruin everything? " Andraste hissed angrily.

"When's the initiation?

- Tonight.

- The Caste is worried. The Hizaion lands have sunk even more into Faraoh's shadow.

- You should know, he's your master.

- He is not!"

The elf clenched fists. He had to explain. Who he was, why he had come into the forest— the real reason. He needed to explain his feelings. But she wouldn't let him. Her anger made her deaf to any explanation.

"Tonight, I'll be here. I'll watch over you. I promise.

- And then? What will you do with the *other?* The *other me* that destroys the forest?

- What are you doing with an elf? "

It was Hal who'd joined them. How long had he been listening?

"He's... a friend. A friend of Etheldrede.

- After the way you talked to him, I wouldn't want to be your friend.

- Were you looking for me, Hal? Andraste asked, annoyed.

- We have a workshop to start. "

By the time Andraste turned, Lyander had already disappeared. Hal swayed on his feet.

"Maybe I should tell the Sages that you received a visit.

- Maybe." She let slip nonchalantly.

Seeing how little hold he had on the situation, the young man turned up his charm.

"There are few stories about elves that joined with mortals. But they exist. Do you want me to tell you my favorite? "

Andraste didn't even bother to answer and quickened her pace to reach the clearing. Beeja looked worried, but Andraste smiled peacefully. Andraste really enjoyed her company. It was the first time she'd met a girl her age. She hoped they would have time to talk. Wyre gave the instructions to the entire group:

"Form a circle. Link your Heka and find the crystals."

The novices looked at each other, surprised and bewildered. They had never done any exercise of this kind.

"Come on. You have all the tools. Breathing, visualizations, you can even use an invocation or incantation if you like…" Wyre encouraged.

Agaric, much harsher, said:

"How will you cope when you are alone, poor, with the sheer force of your mind to get you out of a situation? Come on! Show us what the latest generation of apprentice sorcerers, priests, and lightworkers can do! "

Stung by these words, they did just that. They closed their eyes, synchronised their breath, and then directing their fingertips to the earth, they became magnets. Sucking all the energy from the earth, they tried to make it vibrate.

But nothing moved. Not a single blade of grass. They had to succeed! Andraste exhaled with more force, and inhaled, opening every pore of her skin, letting her spinal column undulate to the rhythm of her breathing. Her body that breathed in *Heka*. Beeja and others began to imitate her, timidly, following her rhythm. She could maybe raise her power by just a notch. Just a notch. Just what was needed, despite the little strength she had left after last night.

Beeja and Hal began to sweat, trembling. Holding their concentration at such tension between body and earth seemed above their strength. Only Andraste and Dehir resisted. Now it was the body which was set in motion, solidly anchored to the ground by their feet, from their belly up to their neck. It was like a raw and instinctive dance, which allowed them to express themselves. Andraste maintained concentration. They saw little by little all the pebbles and gravel turn below them. The earth was alive and working, and answered their silent appeal.

The crystals then emerged, silent and triumphant stars scattered on the ground. Andraste was suddenly moved. These crystals were a painful reminder of the teachings of Lyra, and her presence sorely lacking in her life. Was she proud of her?

"The rise of the crystals is the ascension of your being: the stones that appeared will meet your needs. Keep them on you. Take them and love them," Kunrun told them.

"More power, through more awareness," Wyre said in a firm voice.

Andraste had obtained a basalt of kunzite, and a silicon stone. Beeja blew on a quartz, which allowed for contact with the fairies. Hal had obtained a sugilite and an imperial topaz stone of wisdom. Dehir slipped an iron eye in his bag, supposed to revitalize the spirit and vitality, and a tiger eye to rule out external emotional projections. Andraste remained thoughtful: she received three stones. Three stones was a lot. Would they serve her successively or throughout her life?

The three Sages had returned to the fire. Andraste exchanged a smile with the other novices. Despite their differences, and their personalities, of course, they had succeeded. They mutually congratulated each other, smiling before returning to the fire.

"We'll now have a class before returning to the foyer for the initiation," began Agaric.

Do you have any questions? You can ask what you want. "

It was Dehir who began:

"What does the Caste do today? And the Council?

- Initially the Council was composed of demi-gods, the priests of the very first Sabians. It is they who asked the elves hundreds and hundreds of years ago to serve the kings and let them lead this human world. The elves had reigned enough. It was time for peace between humans and magical races. Humans, guided by elves lead different magical kingdoms very wisely. Kingdoms of humans, animals, plants and minerals. This is a board that directs the rest of the priests. The Council had a close relationship with the royal family. Today, we try to give the magic of Hizaion back in other ways that we owe them. We are much more involved in the research and training of priests than before. The head of the previous Council was unable to detect the right people, preferring political affairs and a very strict organization of the caste, rather than focusing on training. It was a serious mistake. We also have a mission to find all the prophecies of old and study them. That was the second mistake of the previous Council. "

At these words, Andraste's ears pricked up. Beeja asked:

"What are *Yatras?* I mean, no one has explained to us how we got here this morning.

- The *Yatra* is a complex and high-level practice. A level you reach later, much later. The trips, including body and mind, can only be performed by members of the Council.

- But how did you manage to take us with you? "

Agaric's laugh rang clear and frank, slapping his knee with the palm of his hand:

"Because we are Sages, very dear Beeja!"

He smiled protectively now, while she blushed in her hemp hat for her question that was between insolence and naivety. Hal cleared his throat:

"What is absolute power?"

Agaric was now puffing on a pipe. His eyes in the flames, he clicked his tongue, taking a drag of his pipe, and knitting his eyebrows.

"Absolute power for a priest is to always control his thoughts and emotions. Instinctively, naturally. Humility and openness to the unknown and what is to come is a necessary quality to the absolute fulfilment of which you speak. But few people have this quality ... We need a spirit of adventure, and a well-organized mind. Going beyond the techniques is a question of attitude. "

Hal pursed his lips, looking down on the embers: this was clearly not the answer he expected.

"Tell us about the power of crystals please, master." Andraste had reflected on her first question. She didn't want to seem abrupt.

"Quartz is the most powerful, the most pure. A legend says that it is the same star, the same fragment of a daughter star of the Orion sun, far from our world. The stars resonate with us, in one way or another. In the infinitely small as in the infinitely large. In our thoughts, our actions, our emotions.

- Did you use Quartz to come? "

Wyre smiled at Agaric.

"Yes we used quartz's force of attraction to arrive."

She pulled out a quartz disk the size of her palm, shining in the night, from her immaculate shirt. Agaric pulled out a piece of quartz twice the size of his thumb, and Kunrun went to his indefinable form.

"Our quartz resonates with that which exists in the forest.

- Where is this crystal? Hal asked feverishly.

- Hidden in the primitive temple of Hizaion. It protects Etheldrede. And we protect it. This will also be your mission. "

Andraste took a breath and asked the question that had been burning her lips since morning.

"What is the prophecy?

At these words, she looked intently at Agaric.

"There are many prophecies...

- That of the destroyer. "

An icy silence fell upon them.

"This prophecy was fulfilled four decades ago, by Faraoh! Kunrun cut in.

- Cassandra and Aygulf don't appear to share this view."

Wyre, so sweet and even-tempered, glared with her black eyes. Andraste knew she stirred painful memories, but it was now or never.

"They're not the only ones," Agaric finally whispered after a few minutes.

The Sage looked at him offended, while Kunrun tried to adjust his position against the branches. The situation was uncomfortable. They were not supposed to stray this far from their teachings, and they shouldn't show signs of disagreement within the Council... It was the disunity and power struggles that destroyed the older generation of priests. They didn't need to repeat history.

"You don't need to know the prophecy as a whole, but know that in a few words, it's this: a being will come to destroy the world and rebuild it. But there's a translation problem. And we don't have it all. "

Andraste hung on his every word.

"And." "And" can also be translated as "or" in the Sabian language.

- So this is a Sabian prophecy?

- Yes. "

Wyre rose, dusting herself off and declared:

"Well, this session is over. We'll end this initiation with a meditation of an hour and we'll return to the foyer. This is the time to integrate all the knowledge you've absorbed, and to prepare yourself mentally for your initiation tonight." Andraste and Agaric were left alone as everyone went off to find a place to rest. She murmured:

"So according to you, the destroyer is yet to come.

- It's already here in my opinion. "

Andraste felt her mouth become dry. Should she continue this slippery dialogue, or should she leave? In truth, she wanted to escape at any cost. But Agaric and his sparkling eyes nailed her to the spot.

"You also have a medallion.

- How do you know? She asked bravely.

- I don't need to know. I have this incredible gift typically human: intuition.

Andraste took out her medallion. She felt as though she were naked in front of the Sage. It was her most precious and intimate possession. The only thing she held of her mother. Her only link.

"It protects you. You know that, don't you? Instinctively. "

Andraste nodded.

"It is like a mirror. Look at it when you lose your way. It'll bring you back. "

Andraste then noticed that Agaric mechanically clutched the satchel he held at his side in his hand. He'd now slipped his hand inside. Her heart panicked. Was there a dagger? Was that the purpose of the caste? Was he going to eliminate her coldly? She felt her blood quicken in the veins of her temples. No. She couldn't transform now! She shook her medallion more, clinging to the cold metal to remain herself.

"Andraste!"

The clear and trembling voice of Beeja stopped her flow of thoughts.

"Andraste, you must be exhausted. I've prepared you a bed of leaves close to mine. "

Andraste exhaled deeply and smiled, stood up, bowed to Agaric and joined Beeja. They took a few quick steps towards the woods. Beeja suddenly took her hand, and whispered:

"You can't talk to a sage alone, Andraste. That's not how it's done! "

Andraste was stunned.

"There's a hierarchy to respect, and codes..."

Beeja stopped contemplating her comrade who watched numbly.

"Cassandra never told you that?

- Well ... no, she focused on other things. I studied a lot more botany, that's for sure," said Andraste, uncomfortably.

"Well we always sit in a circle around the priests and sages. We try to sit up straight, with our hands forming a circle or a triangle. It is a sign of receptivity—you show that you are ready to learn."

They had arrived at their leafy beds. Unfortunately, there were nettles. Beeja still had some progress to make in botany. But Andraste said nothing, and simply thanked her. Beeja continued her lesson, happy to teach Andraste something and to bond with her.

"Always present your palms open. Your nails, your hair, your skin, and your body should be clean. No jewellery, no sign of individuality. You serve the light. You are above that. "

Beeja's voice grew excited.

"How long have you been a novice for?

- Ho, I think I've always been one my heart. But I entered into service at the age of fifteen. And you?

- Well, I was born here ... It just happened naturally."

Beeja's naiveté and faith were refreshing. She was pure. Andraste wondered how many young apprentices, novices and priestesses, as innocent as Beeja, had been raped and murdered sixteen years ago.

"Andraste... How... How did you know what to do for the crystals?

- Intuition," said Andraste.

Beeja leaned her pretty head to the side.

"After a wild ride in the forest, I feel like I need to breathe through every limb of my body to recover my *Heka*. My lungs alone aren't enough. And I think my body felt that it needed even more of it to bring forth the crystals. I think we should have more confidence in our body. Isn't illness a sign that something isn't right inside of us?

- I admire you, Andraste. So many things seem natural for you.

- Believe me Beeja, I would like your insight. Your faith also. "

Beeja blushed with pleasure at her remark.

"Beeja, do you know Aman well?

- Yes, well, especially Hal who's working closely with him on this trip, but it was he who found me in Rosendal.

- I need your help, Beeja. "

The girl looked at her now, anxiously.

"You see, I want to become a healer. And I recorded all my notes in a notebook. Handwritten notes, lessons from Cassandra ... I mean, it's very important to me.

- The book Aman took from you this morning.

178

- I need to recover it. There is so much to know in it. I don't understand why he took it from me.

- But he's just curious about your training...

- I don't think he'll give it back to me, Beeja.

- And you want me to get it back...

- How would you react if someone stole the memory of the past three years, Beeja. Your life, your dreams, your mission ... All this, taken away. "

At these words Beeja, paled. Andraste had touched something inside of her.

"I'll do what I can."

Andraste took her in his arms to thank her, got up and walked away. She felt Beeja observe her with curiosity, but Andraste felt better. She trusted her. Suddenly she heard moans and muffled footsteps in dead leaves. She crouched on the floor, underneath a bush, and crawled toward the sound. What she saw left her stunned.

Chapter 14

Kunrun stood entwined with Dehir, kissing passionately. The Sage and the novice repressed their moaning, and struggled not to let themselves go on the floor. Kunrun stroked the young man's face, tracing it with his slender and inquisitive fingers, while Dehir, his head slightly thrown back, gave way to the ecstasy of embrace and kisses of his master. Andraste, stunned, was petrified. Kunrun took the young man in his arms, stroking his head and sighed:

"We live in strange times, Dehir ... In my day, there was a real selection.

- What do you mean, Oh wise Kunrun?

- I mean, you probably would have been the only one initiated today. You have so much talent.

- It is you master, who taught me everything! The *Heka* flows through you like a fountain. You are my fountain of life ... Dehir exclaimed.

- Shhh, I know, I know I shouldn't... But I feel so much potential in you..."

The priest gazed languidly at the emaciated features his lover, giving caresses to which Dehir responded with passionate kissing. He held him, refusing the limits of their body as if he wanted melt into him. Kunrun gently took his hands and pulled away, whispering:

"When you come into the tunnel, ask for the help of the elements. Ask to be guided: to the east, you invoke Yul, for the south, you ask assistance from Ethil, to the west, Iglal and to the north, Shaïe ... do you understand? "

What cheating! Andraste had felt a moment of illegitimacy against the other novices; she was so lucky to grow up with Cassandra that she felt guilty. But now, she was shocked. A relationship between priests and apprentices was forbidden. What about a novice with Sage, a master! It rendered his teaching biased and uneven. But the novice continued:

"The girl intrigues me. She isn't normal. "

- Don't worry. According to her design we showed Aman, she's entirely inappropriate for our caste. But Aman thinks she can bring power to our cause. She has powers for sure.

- What do you mean by inadequate? "

Andraste, under the low branches, tried to retreat, but a branch snapped under her foot. They separated, frightened, sweeping the surrounding area with their glances. The Sage's regard crossed that of Andraste. She spun around to return to Beeja. It was Dehir who caught her by the arm:

"You won't say anything, will you?

- I don't even know what I saw," said Andraste, embarrassed, continuing her route with great strides.

- I love him. Not like a human. I mean... He's given me so much. He gives me strength. It's not what you believe... Well, it's more than you think, anyway.

- This has nothing to do with me!" She hurled at him.

She fled from him. She wanted to erase the image from her memory. If the other sages knew, Dehir and Kunrun would both be excluded, banished. It wasn't what she wanted. She wanted to be inducted and to be assigned a mission. That's what she wanted. She wanted to leave and go to Etheldrede to fulfil her destiny ... If she had one. She wanted answers to her questions: why does she transform, what exactly is the power of the medallion ... Could she control this thing? She wanted to destroy this creature that lived within her. And it suddenly occurred to her that the only one who seemed to hold the key to these enigmas was the Tengu. She had to see it again. She stopped in her tracks, trying to make out a faint silhouette leaning against a tree. It was Agaric. The Sage dozed in his black beard. Andraste walked around the tree, slowly, surely. She had an idea. She knelt and put her hand in Agaric's satchel. She wanted to know what he was keeping in there. If it was a dagger or poison. She introduced a finger, then another, and spread the cords. The bag was now gaping. Agaric didn't move. His long arms hung along his amorphous body, as he moved his lips. He always seemed to repeat the same name.

Andraste felt something under her fingers:

"Okri..." called Agaric.

The young novice was doing everything to control her breathing. She had to know. There was something important in this piece of leather, she knew it.

She was holding something. Something sharp. But as her hand closed around it, Agaric's hand closed around on her wrist. Terrified, she dared not move, breathless. But Agaric just drew out his hand to observe what she'd taken.

"Insolent, disobedient, gifted and curious, he said.

- Excuse me master. I...

- This is *mordenite*. This substance can kill you or save your life.

- Why do you have it on you?

- Because I wanted absolute power you see..."

Agaric looked sad now. He released her hand and grabbed the vial.

"After forty years of wandering between cities, the Caste has progressively dissolved. Some have simply dropped out of the order. Others... had to hide within the population. I had a wife and a daughter. My daughter got sick. I thought my hands could heal her. But my gift ... I developed it, I worked to the extreme. To the point that I lost myself. Without being able to heal my daughter, Okri. I suffer because of this gift. And I sought for years anything that could heal me. That is why I'm a master healer and master poisoner.

- The *mordenite*, could it heal someone…possessed? "

Agaric looked at her thoughtfully. He plunged his hand into his pocket and handed her a vial an inch high.

He was so strange: a mixture of benevolence and fierce independence. Did he know about the monster who lived within her? It was impossible. But without a doubt he had detected her abnormality. Suddenly, the thud of a bowl being knocked vibrated in the air. Andraste grabbed the jar and found herself running to the other novices. Dehir and Kunrun ignored her, but the young novice was visibly uncomfortable. He remained close to Wyre and Hal dutifully dusting his clothes, and avoiding her gaze.

Without a word, the troops started walking. It was time for them to complete their trials.

For the first time in seventeen years, the hatch covered with the carpet in the middle of the dining room was opened, and Andraste went down into the crypt beneath the house. It was a large dark and damp room, with bluish slabs coming from Southeast winds of Yelm. Cassandra had heated and lighted crypt with torches as soon as the Sages had left with the novices.

Naked on the stone table, the novices were coated with oil by Aygulf, Ferens, and Cassandra. Then they rubbed their skin with rice powder mixed with apple seed powder. They smeared them with mud, and then scraped their skin with pruning hooks. Andraste felt her skin crunch under Cassandra's sure hands. She closed her eyes, seeing her old life fall away with the dead skin. Pain didn't exist.

She was revamped. She no longer felt like herself. She was going to be an apprentice. Serving the goddess. Serving a more just world. A light worker. She remembered the moments spent in the forest, Lyander, Lyra. The memories paraded in her head. She opened her eyes and saw Cassandra's face framed by dark, red hair. It looked a crown. The girl had a thought about her guardian: with patience and love, she had tried to form and shape her mind, just as she had sculpted her body with the sickle tonight.

They girded their loins with a white loincloth, and the girls had their breasts bandaged. They braided their hair back to hinder any movement, and were led individually to a trapdoor. Everyone would go into the foundations of the crypt and follow his or her own path.

Aman, beautiful in his white and red ritual dress, had planted his stick and said:

"Once inside, you can't turn back. We'll close doors behind you. You can only advance and face your fears. Go and meet the deity and give Her honor and let Her guide you to the exit. "

During his speech, Agaric painted a cross on each of their backs with olibanum oil. He followed the line of their spines and drew a horizontal line, on the line below the shoulder blades. Arriving behind Andraste, Agaric let his hands linger on her back, warming her with his hands. The girl thanked him mentally. Everything would be okay. She pressed her tongue in her mouth: she'd rolled the medallion in its chain and hid it in her cheek. At that moment, more than ever, she wanted to feel close to her mother.

The priests lifted the flagstones. A fetid air escaped. Beeja trembled on her right. Andraste looked at Cassandra and smiled. She wanted to honor her. She took this picture before going down into the underground. Whatever awaited her, she was ready.

She landed in a stream, which ploughed the ground. Which way to go? She spat her locket in her hand and slipped it into her loincloth. She chose to leap forward, and back along the creek. It would lead to the river. Andraste felt her heart swell, exalted. She hoped Beeja, with her fragile constitution, would pass the test.

She continued her pilgrimage, dimly lit by meagre torches, hesitantly moving along the slippery on wet stones. The passage became narrower. She thanked Lyra mentally, for her training that had sculpted her body and fortified her mind.

She noticed that she walked silently, instinctively. Suddenly, she came out into a room with high walls and votive columns. A mist surrounded her... Several tunnels opened into the room. Were all the novices supposed to pass through them? She listened carefully, but didn't hear any other footsteps than her own. She was alone. She crossed the room, hardly daring to lift her feet. Andraste didn't know why, but she felt the need to get low to the ground. She didn't like the idea of being seen without being able to see. The stench was becoming unbearable ... She carried on and perceived an air current to her right. This must be the way out.

She progressed like a spider, slowly and surely, her legs and arms folded. She rushed into the tunnel and gave a little sigh of relief. The air smelled of roses now.

She continued in the tunnel, darker this time, which led her to an enchanting and disturbing vision. It was a cave, a bullet-shaped cavity. The infiltration of water from the river had dug furrows like in the curves of a woman, while the floor slabs had been submerged. On the sides, snakes painted with red earth slithered along the furrows, gravity-resistant, hiding in moist, dark crevices and following the strange contoured spirals carved into the rock by priests several hundred years ago... Andraste lowered herself gently into the icy water, exhaling loudly to withstand thermal shock. It was as if her skin was pierced by a thousand needles.

At the back, housed in an oval alcove, stood the statue of Dana, immaculate and unreal in this setting. Surrounded by shells, fern leaves, nut shells, crystals and gold dust, she reigned over the depths of the earth, the majestic and gentle mother of all wealth and abundance.

Andraste crossed the waters, struggling against the water pressure around her shoulders. Arriving before the goddess, she prayed. She thanked her for everything, all the tests, all the trials that she'd undertaken so far, her induction tonight. Tomorrow she would be an apprentice. She would have powers which would then be developed and placed at the service of the community, and to the service of the goddess. She traced the energy lines of *Heka* with her saliva on the statue. It was time to emerge. She slipped between snakes through the tunnel behind the statue. Andraste for a moment contemplated the face of the Mother of all. She was also her mother. It was perhaps her that she had sought all these years.

She climbed on the rock to the crypt. She froze, struck by a cry. It was Beeja. In the upper part of the crypt, the priests looked dumbfounded. Cassandra feared the worst. A novice had never died during initiation. What was he going on in the depths of the earth?

Blood. Andraste passed through the mist as she entered the room. Beeja had clearly struggled before giving up. Hiero was holding her between his claws and drank her blood.

"Approach," whispered Hiero, abandoning Beeja.

Andraste was half naked, and her only weapon that of her medallion. She had no chance. Beeja's body rolled over. Andraste approached her and felt that she had a pulse, but it was weak. She was breathing weakly, but she was alive.

Something was wrong. Hiero wasn't breathing normally. He crawled to the wall while Andraste watched, half kneeling. He had lost a lot of blood since last night in the temple. She'd foraged so deep into his muscles that his wound never closed. She wondered if she ran off with Beeja's body, if he'd still have the strength to pursue them.

"You'll excuse me for your little sister, but I needed to regain strength. We haven't finished, you and me.

- It all ends tonight. "

Hiero broke into a throaty laugh that echoed dismally in the moist room.

"Oh no ... no my dear. It all starts tonight. You have no idea of the fate that awaits you."

Time went on, and Beeja's blood would regenerate Hiero within minutes—the two novices could not escape him.

"I can help you accomplish your mission. I have the answers to the questions that haunt you.

- What are you talking about?

- You want to know who you creator is? "

Tengu's words echoed in her head. Yes, she wanted to know where she came from. Was Hiero related to her birth? Did he know things that could help her control her metamorphosis? The game was worth playing…

"What do you want from me?

- Your blood ... and your help when the time comes..."

Andraste looked stunned.

"We are naturally allies, little novice. Since your birth, in fact.

- What do you mean?

- Give me your arm. "

Hiero looked exhausted.

"Tell me first ... I have no faith in your word."

Hiero exhaled a groan of exhaustion and annoyance.

"I had an ally who betrayed me in the Battle of Goiri. Defeated, I entered the forest just before the Azur fell. I followed the trace of the human chosen to give birth to Faraoh's creature, your father, your creator. "

Tengu's words were like a dagger in Andraste's heart. She articulated with difficulty:

"No... you're not telling the truth...

- No matter what I say ... You'll see for yourself. You're his

creature, his thought, designed and created by him for his purposes. "

And suddenly, Hiero leapt forward and grabbed Andraste's hair. He suddenly thrust his jaw in her neck, and brought forth blood from her jugular vein. Andraste uttered a cry of pain, when lightning seemed to strike him. She strangled the creature, plunging her fingers in his still oozing flesh. She pushed with all her might on top of the wound reactivating the blood stream.

Hiero released her and arched in pain. She then bent down and hooked him with her leg. Hiero fell on his back, slipping on the wet ground, breaking a wing, and screaming in rage.

Andraste grabbed Beeja, who was fortunately light, and slung her across her shoulder, running towards the opening, slipping on the stones. She chose to go along the submerged basin and skirted the walls, disturbing the snakes, clinging to crevices on her shaking legs. She felt the blood dripping from her shoulder from Beeja's soaked and shivering body. Finally, she came up behind the statue, and rushed into the tunnel, throwing her last ounce of strength in her race.

Chapter 15

After climbing out, she realized she was in the clearing, standing before the primitive temple. The tomb of Hizaion. They looked at her, bloodied, exhausted, panting, as she deposited the weight on her shoulders on the ground. Andraste stumbled and fell to her knees, ready to spit up her lungs. She'd pushed her body to the limits.

Agaric rushed to support her, while Cassandra looked after Beeja. She opened her eyes and murmured vaguely:

"She saved me. She gave him her blood ... the Tengu. They made a pact ... She saved me. "

Ferens leapt forward and spat:

You see! Aman, I told you! I felt it! This girl is unworthy! Nobody knows where she came from! She reeks of traitors and the Shadow!

Andraste was struck by so much violence. Aman watched the scene with an anxious eye. Silence reigned. Agaric gave Andraste a vial with a green liquid to drink. She caught her breath and stood up. She was determined to fight this idiot, but Aman raised his hand and said:

"We must continue the initiation."

Agaric gave Beeja the same potion while Cassandra wrapped a bandage around her shoulder with trembling hands. Ferens, Aygulf, Hal and Dehir closed the stone slabs while Wyre and Aman murmured softly.

The novices were each placed on a stone, and were again washed by priests, this time with water. A fresh, soothing water. But instead of indulging in this moment of pleasure, Andraste's brain was boiling. She would have to defend herself before the Council, to Cassandra, to the other novices. She felt anger rising in her, and despair. No, not now. She now could not fail after all she had been through.

Each novice was naked and anointed with lavender oil. Then Cassandra, Ferens Aygulf clothed them in the traditional *baya* garment: a brown belt, called a *Tobu*, a shirt, and wide black pants they could that they tucked into their boots. Then they clothed them in *kara*, the sleeveless coat caps. They each received a new *athame*, their ritual knife engraved with their name and a dagger made from the tip of a broken sword, a *sylan*, which they strapped to their thigh with a leather strap. They then received the *sporran*, a leather pocket for their instruments and books.

It was now time for the *bjotee*, the ceremony of light, and the oath. Hal, Dehir and Beeja each made the same movement to each priest holding a candle in front of their chest. They symbolically

194

caught the light of the candle in the palm of their hands and bowed their heads, placed it in front of them and then to their mouths. The priests, meanwhile, spread rose petals on their heads. Andraste closed her eyes chanting with them:

"I am an unlimited being, with unlimited powers, connected to an infinite source ... I ask to turn hate into force, fear into love, doubt into faith, and to transmute me into light. As servant of the light, I'll become the light. "

Cassandra then came to Andraste. It was time. She was predestined. She had been waiting for this all her childhood. All these trials, all those nights in the dark and the silence of the forest, dreaming of the world of oblivion and missions that would be entrusted to her. Cassandra, her protectress smiled benevolently. She too had waited for this day. This moment which was the culmination of years of teaching—it made her proud. Andraste began to dream of her specialty. Would she become a potions' expert like Agaric, or try her hand at crystals? A scarf of a particular color would be added to her traditional clothing at the end of her training. Yes, she would honor Cassandra. But Aman's icy voice sounded:

"Veto."

Stunned, Cassandra turned. The wise old man kept an unreadable expression while Ferens smiled with satisfaction.

"A wise decision," he agreed.

But Aman cut in:

"Silence. I'm simply postponing her initiation. We need to know more about her and her story. "

Andraste was shocked. Her whole body rose, and she poured out all her resentment:

"But you know all about me! Cassandra knows everything about me! "

Andraste had started screaming, furiously.

"We know that this isn't true. You have a very independent character. You have a taste for secrecy. You ask a lot of questions about the other world from your childhood. Are you really ready to join our cause? Are you really who you claim to be? "

Andraste clenched her fists, trembling. She pursed her lips and the blood left her face under the charge. Aman continued:

"You will leave with us. You will study in the city of Rosendal, and we will see your profile and abilities. Look at this as a natural extension of your education here. Maybe Cassandra gave you too much too soon before she actually understood who she had in front of her.

- She's our only hope! "Cassandra said, with vehemence.

- We have three hopes right in front of us: healthy, skilled, and worthy of the Caste," said Kunrun placidly

They were leagued against her. Even Wyre and Aygulf said nothing and remained silent.

"You close your mind to your tutor, you spawn with an elf, a Daikini, and now, this creature! Are you even still a virgin? Why did you give him your blood? "

Andraste was staring at him now, eyes black with anger and hatred.

"It's true, I should have let the creature kill Beeja."

Ferens watched in amazement. She pronounced the words with cynicism and coldness. Cassandra was aghast. Andraste had an idea: she took out her Anjara medal she held tightly in the palm of her hand, and put it jauntily around her neck. At the sight of this, the four sages stood up, and the priests backed away. Even Cassandra looked at Andraste, dazed. It was as if she didn't recognize her. Wyre stepped forward, frightened:

"Are you the child of destruction? Are you the one that will destroy the temple, all that's left of magic?

- I don't know. I know you've made me angry. And you will regret it. You will regret not giving me my chance today.

- An Anjara medallion! Thief! Insolent rebel! Unworthy bitch! "

Ferens spat in her face and tried to grab her medallion in his hand. Andraste used the levitation spell:

"Barnasa! Leutyae! Bucella!"

But her voice vibrated with anger and Ferens was thrown back in a cry of pain. He fell like a crumpled puppet in the dust.

Andraste felt his heart beat faster—her spell had exceeded her will. Would she lose control of herself? Would she turn again? Her anger gave her the taste of blood in her mouth. Yet, she heard herself speak with irony and a calm tone:

"You don't want to let a kid participate in your great quest to save your world? You're right. I am anything but a kid. I'm better than all of you combined. The medallion is mine, mine and mine alone. Whatever its power, prophecy or not, with or without your help, in the name of its legacy, I will choose my destiny and the means which I will use to resurrect magic."

She could no longer stop the venom of her words. The Sages and priests retreated, frightened by so much violence. Even the forest was silent. Andraste left, drunk with anger and pride.

It was all her frustration, fed for years, which had surfaced. And her transformation that night had hurt, deep in her being:

"You are nothing but frightened sheep! Hypocrites! At least one of you has broken his vow of chastity! And you demand respect!"

198

Dehir swallowed and fixed his gaze the floor. But Kunrun shot her a murderous glance. She continued, taking pleasure now in provoking them. Now she had the chance to humiliate them:

"You didn't know fight this battle even though you had the opportunity. You want to submit to your stupid laws? You have no choice! I'm your only hope! Despite their qualities, not a single novice here could destroy the Tengu in combat! No one! I've survived its attack three times! There is none that could master the magic I possess, and knows in her flesh, what true *Heka* is! You're right: I'm not on your side! "

Andraste turned and left them there. Even Agaric couldn't bring her back. She'd made her decision. Cassandra, pale, ran and caught her by the arm

"You're crazy! My word! Where are you going? Come back! "

But Andraste, cold as stone, said:

"Thank you, Cassandra. For everything. But I do not have time for the approval of those old fearful and senile priests. I have nothing to do in your Caste. I know that now.

- Pride blinds you Andraste!

- It is you who are blind.

- Andraste, don't turn your back on the Caste: it is they who can decide your powers, your access to the status as a healer, a priestess... They're the makers of our caste, but also our protectors! "

Andraste hesitated, then turned, looking into her eyes, and said:

"I won't disappoint you Cassandra, but it's my own camp I choose today."

Cassandra pulled out her wand:

"Andraste ... do not force me to do this."

She didn't give her time. Andraste affixed her hands in front of her and released a discharge of *Heka*. The body of the healer flew backwards and collapsed onto Aman.

Andraste ran breathlessly to return to the foyer. She climbed the stairs four at a time, and prepared her bag. She had to get out as quickly as possible. She tore through her room but didn't find the book Aman had taken. What an unworthy scum: he must have kept it. She put her healing instruments in her leather pouch, some herbs, food, a copper bowl and a stick, crystals, some clothes, and Lyander's sword. She hesitated to take a few books but she was out of time. And it would have been theft. She was not a thief. Just ... a rebel who had ransacked a ritual and spat in the face of the Sages...

She was now running through the plain: she had to reach the limits of the forest of Etheldrede quickly, through the Azur, the sacred dome. If the priests caught up to her, what would they do? If she were really the "destroyer," would they try to eliminate her? The girl kept her eyes fixed on the sky. But how to break through? Hiero said she'd need her medallion to get to the other side, to find her people ... Suddenly, she felt herself lifted from the ground by her collar. Lyander perched on his mount, a huge black deer. Andraste, surprised, wondered if he'd witnessed her initiation. And yet there he was, faithful and loyal to his oath.

When they arrived at the border, the sunlight had changed. Or was it the place that was special? The waves of different colors roamed the translucent walls of the dome. It was a powerful magic, ancient, irrigated for decades. They came down from the mount. The black stag nodded in a noble air, before returning to the west. Andraste stepped forward but before she could touch the wall, Lyander grabbed her arm. He removed his medallion and pressed it against the wall. But he pulled back and said:

"You're crazy. Courageous, irresponsible, and strong. You might be the one of the prophecy. Or not. But I believe in you. I will follow you everywhere. And I'll protect you. "

The girl, in a silent thanks, put her hand on of Lyander's shoulder. They stood silently smiling at each other. She didn't know the nature of her feelings for him, but he fascinated her, and she trusted him.

"What will you do?"

Andraste looked at the tip of her shoes, and her outfit. An apprentice received a mission, an action to perform, after two additional years of education. Alone, without support of the Caste, she could only rely on her audacity.

"Organize resistance: from the people, without the Caste. Defeat Faraoh. Save the lands of Hizaion from his claws, and restore all magic. What's your opinion?

- It's a good plan. Beyond the ambition and madness…I like it! And I see you haven't forgotten my sword!" Said the elf.

They laughed both. Lyander realized how similar they were: they were lonely, ambitious, and made no concessions to anyone. She attracted him, without knowing if it was love, a protective instinct toward humans, or a deep friendship. A friendship as he would have had with a brother in arms. The girl with golden hair restored his hope. She restored his faith in the face of possible enemy resistance of Faraoh. And her monstrous nature, he had to admit…It fascinated him. He didn't see the creature in her, but the power, unsuspected, housed in this frail woman's body just waiting to hatch.

"Andraste!"

The girl and the elf returned. Beeja cut through the tall grass, her complexion reddened from running, breathless, followed by Agaric. It was he who began:

202

"I guess I have no way to convince you to follow me to Rosendal?

- No.

- Even though I'm your master? I'll teach you everything I know, Andraste. You wouldn't be accountable to anyone. "

His words were attractive. Agaric, even if he wasn't psychic, could read their hearts. He understood her thirst for knowledge. Yet she heard herself reply:

"No agaric. I can't wait anymore. I must find answers to my questions. About me. About my origins. I have more work than the Caste could even give me.

- Then must you succeed, Andraste. It is necessary that future generations of priests and novices hear about the day when a novice succeeded her induction, and then shouted at the Council! "

Andraste bit her lips in shame: she respected Agaric, of course, and it certainly was not him she was talking about when she talked about being old and senile. She felt close to him—they were not part of the Caste. Something, personality and destiny had brought them together. But Agaric laughed for the first time. Beeja, was still staring at Andraste with panicked eyes.

"Andraste, thank you for saving me ... Sorry, I led the Caste astray. I don't mean ... Are you sure of what you are doing?

- You spoke the truth, Beeja. I know what I have to do and I'll find a way. "

The girl was touched by the emotion of Beeja. She took her right hand gently and covered it with her left hand. The young apprentice smiled shyly. She withdrew her hand hastily, and pulled a book out of her satchel:

"My book!" Cried Andraste. She pulled Beeja to her, and held her tightly in her arms. She felt her frail body panicked like a bird barely recovered from her emotions.

"Thank you, Beeja. And do not worry, we'll meet again. I know we'll meet again.

- When you are on the other side, go to Imani. It's an old tavern. I don't know what neighborhood you'll land in, but it's in the ancient city of Samatya. Imani is a refuge, a place of passage ... for people like us. "

The Elf stared Agaric down. Had they met before? Agaric continued:

"Since you interrupted the ceremony, you never got your name. But know that I would have given you one of *Raksadrista*.

- What does it mean?

- It's Sabian. It means, *sentinel of the invisible*. Who is the master, who is the apprentice? Novices, apprentices, priests, or Sages, only the one that is open to the messages of the invisible, and beyond, will fulfill his destiny. Do you know why I gave you that name?

- To contain my bad temper?

- This is how the first priestesses were called, who were women only. They were the Sentinels of the Invisible. Sentinels sent to this earth to protect and serve. No one can become a servant of the Light and a Sage, if they aren't first a Sentinel of the Invisible. If your fate is linked to that of this world, then this name can guide you. And protect you. For the Caste does not forgive those who dare to deviate from the path carved out for them. We will meet again, Andraste. I hope you will have done great things when the time comes. "

Andraste turned to the other apprentice:

"And you, Beeja, what's your name?

- *Adistara*. Innocence..."

They both smiled. Andraste stepped back, savoring one last look at Etheldrede Forest, which had been her home since birth. She had a feeling, stronger than ever, she that she would again cross Hiero, the Tengu on her path, because he was the one who was able to reveal her nature to the detriment of Lyra and Lyander. She looked for Morphnée, but he didn't come. She thought about her mother, who was based here, Lyra. Both had given their lives for her. For the hope she represented. She suppressed the tears that rose, turning away, feeling so small suddenly. And disarmed. Lyander laid his hand on her shoulder. It was him, her only support now. Yet by probing his crazy and wild eyes, she knew she did not need a protector. She needed to believe in her as much as her mother, Lyra, Cassandra, and Agaric believed in her. She would have the answers to her questions and she would find out who she was. She started a war with the priestly caste. She held in her a kind of monster she had to learn to control. And the course of her life had taken an unexpected turn. Where was she going? Would the oracles only come to fruition when she began her mission?

Lyander put his hand on her shoulder. Taking a deep breath, she took the chain she had around her neck, and pressed the medallion against the bewitched sphere, passing to the other side.

The journey was brutal, heart-breaking for her body. When she opened her eyes, it was still dark on the other side. Her muscles aching, she looked around her. The city of Samatya was both sublime and worrying. Andraste never could have imagined such a place. Suddenly she panicked: Lyander had disappeared. She was alone. Alone in an unfamiliar world, the world of oblivion.

From the top of the tower 34 1A sector, Agent Reyn thought it was a hallucination. He blinked, looking at the screen of his monitor: two renegades had crossed the frontier of the closed

206

area. He picked up a handset to notify his superior. How was that even possible? Nagos, Captain of the Militia of Renova, director of the Service against the Rebels Sectarian, would not believe it.

Acknowledgements

I would like to thank my family and friends for their support all along the last three years. Thanks to Taylor Smith, Aimee Heriard-Dubreuil, Chloe Sauron for their help in the final step.

Most of all, thank you, dear reader, for starting this journey with Andraste. If you liked the first book, I invite you to like the Facebook page "Memoirs of Hizaion" to keep up with what's next. You can also leave me a note, or email me on my Google+ page.

Please leave a review on GoodReads, or any websitepromoting books. Your opinion matters enormously to me!

Visit facebook for other stories about the Hizaion universe.

Best to you,

D. McNeele

www.ingramcontent.com/pod-product-compliance
Lightning Source LLC
Chambersburg PA
CBHW070118260626
47160CB00004B/1525